THE WAITING GAME

a novella

References:

Scripture taken from The Message. Copyright © 1993, 1994, 1995, 1996, 2000, 2001, 2002. Used by permission of NavPress Publishing Group.

Famuyiwa, R. (Director), Famuyiwa, R., Johnson, I., Heller, P., & Hoffman, T. (Producers), & Elliot, M. (Screenwriter). (2002). *Brown Sugar* [Motion Picture]. United States: Fox Searchlight Pictures.

Edited by Nicole Dorsey

Cover design by Christina Sanders of Cover Girl Graphics, a division of Pretty Flyers Designs.
www.prettyflyers.com
www.covergirlgraphics.com

ISBN-10: 0-692-65033-4
ISBN-13: 978-0-692-65033-2
First Trade Paperback Printing: April 2016
Second Trade Paperback Printing: October 2016

Printed in the US.

Also by Nicole C Diggs
When the Wait Becomes a Weight

www.nicolediggs.com

THE WAITING GAME

a novella

NICOLE C DIGGS

"Every woman has the right and ability to be happy, content, and fulfilled as a single woman."

1

September 13, 2014

"Today's the day. The weather is perfect. All the people I love are patiently awaiting my arrival tonight. My hair looks great. My makeup, well, we'll see how that turns out later. My dress is perfect. It's simple, exactly the way I've always imagined. And it's comfortable. I need to be comfortable tonight. I'm so nervous, but I'm so excited at the same time. I guess knowing with everything in you that something is right for you gives you the peace that you need at a time like this."

April 12, 2014 – 5 months before

"Hey Chivonne! I thought that was you!"

"Oh my goodness! Hey Krystal!" Chivonne screamed, putting down her purse to hug her and waving off the man holding the door to the elevator she was about to get on. "How have you been? I haven't seen you since we graduated eight years ago!"

"I know! It *has* been eight years! I'm great! Everything is good. Good to see you! I almost didn't recognize you with short hair."

"Oh, yeah, I never thought I'd cut my hair, but I'm just trying something different," picking up her purse, tossing it around her shoulder, and running her fingers down the back of her hair, pretending to model in the mirror between the elevator doors. "It's good to see you, too!" looking back at her. "What are you doing here in LA?"

"I'm actually on my honeymoon right now. My *husband* is down in the lobby," Krystal said, gleaming with excitement. "That sounds so weird coming out of my mouth! You remember Darren, don't you?"

"Yes, of course I remember Darren! How could I forget the guy who was always knocking down my dorm room door looking for you, freshman year?"

"That's right! How could I forget that? Sorry about that!"

"No apology necessary! I knew it was only a matter of time before you two tied the knot. So, where are you guys living now? Are you still in North Carolina?"

"We're both in New York now! Darren works in New Jersey and I landed a job in the city, right after graduation, so it worked out perfectly for us."

"That's awesome, Krystal. I'm so happy for you two!"

"Thank you, Chivonne. That means a lot to me. So, what brings *you* here? You're still in Philly, right?" Krystal asked.

"I actually live here now! I moved here about four months ago to open my boutique called The Simple Life; it's just downtown in LA. My family came to visit me this week, but they are leaving today, so I am just seeing them off. My place is way too small to accommodate everyone, so they stayed here at the hotel."

"Wow! That is amazing, Chivonne! You did always talk about your dreams of owning your own business someday. Way to go! Congratulations are definitely in order."

"Thank you! It has been a journey, to say the least, but well worth it. I struggled for years with whether or not to stay at my 9-to-5, or to pursue what I always wanted to do, but it was definitely time to move on. I liked my job, but I just could not see myself working there five or ten years from now, because it wasn't what I'm passionate about, you know?"

"Yeah, I can understand that. Nobody should ever stay at a job, or in anything, that they don't absolutely love doing. Life is way too short for that and God did not give you dreams and talents for them to go unused. But, that had to take a lot of time and traveling back and forth, huh?"

"Oh, absolutely! For several months I traveled back and forth to get everything situated and to make sure that it was the right move for me, and the right *time* to move. Trust me, it was not easy by any means, but it was what I needed to do for myself."

"That's awesome, Chivonne. I know everything will work out amazingly for you, honestly."

"Thanks. I appreciate that, Krystal," pulling her phone out of her purse to look at the time.

"Absolutely! It was good to see you! But, I'm not going to hold you up. I'm sure you've got to get going since you're a successful business owner now!"

"Successful business owner! I like the sound of that!" nodding her head in agreement. "Thank you! And let me get a hug before you go!" Chivonne said, reaching out her arms. "And you enjoy the rest of your honeymoon."

"Oh, thank you girl! I sure will! Good to see you again."

Krystal met her husband in middle school and she always knew she would marry him after both of their careers took off. This wedding was right on schedule. Chivonne always imagined that she would find the love of her life while in school, just like all of her friends did, and be married with at least two kids by now, but that was far from her reality. As a child, she dreamed of having a family of her own and a home for that family to grow in. She often daydreamed of a small, fall-time wedding on a night when the temperature was a perfect blend of warm air and cool winds, a few friends and family members, a fancier-than-necessary reception with great food and too much fun, topped off by a dreamy trip to Paris with her new husband.

Apart from a few classmates here and there, Chivonne never had any real interest in any of the guys she had met in college or at church or work, and none of the guys she had been interested in seemed to show interest in her. Although she did not feel much pressure to be married from close friends and family back home, she was somewhat disappointed that her own plans to be married by now did not pan out.

Being married was something she always wanted for herself. It was the companionship and close friendship, and knowing that there would always be someone standing in her corner, that made her want it so much. With all of her success, she felt like she had no one to share it with, no one to celebrate with, and no one to come home to after a long day's work.

Growing up, Chivonne always admired her grandparents' relationship. Her grandmother on her mother's side boasted of the good man that Chivonne's grandfather was, a kind-hearted man who would do anything for her grandmother, and who was handsome even in his old age. Something that her grandmother once told her when she was just a teenager stuck with her:

"Chivonne, your grandfather snatched me up at the ripe age of twenty-five and he never let go," she remembered. *"Find a man who knows what he wants and that you are it, and never let him get away."*

At 30 years old, Chivonne felt like she had some catching up to do.

After college, Chivonne took a job as a Marketing Assistant at a small firm. Although she had made good money as a recent college grad, she knew it wasn't what she wanted, even after eight years. She ultimately decided to take a risk and move across the country to LA, finally being able to enjoy that perfect warm weather she loved, year round.

Moving to LA meant freedom to her. It was a chance to be completely independent of what she was used to and would force her to step out of her comfort zone to create and live the life she always wanted to live. Making the move required a lot of traveling between Philly and LA, but she was determined to throw caution to the wind and go after her dreams. To finally be in LA, living that dream, was the most exhilarating experience of her life. The last thing she wanted to hear while settling into her new life was that someone else she knew had just gotten married, and she was still single.

In the short few months she had been in LA, Chivonne had met a few guys, like Marcus, the guy who owned the barbershop next door to her boutique. Although Marcus seemed to be a genuine guy, he was recently divorced and was just a little older than she would have liked, not to mention he had a teenage son. She always saw herself being a mother someday, but she wasn't sure that being step-mom to a teenager was where she wanted to start.

And then there was Addison, the muscle-head she met in the frozen food aisle of the grocery store near her apartment. They hit it off well, seeming to have some things in common, like recently moving to LA to start a business. Addison was a fun-loving guy, but turned out to be way too much into his biceps than he was into her.

Moving to LA all alone, where she didn't know too many people, proved to be a tough move, and it sometimes became difficult to make a real connection with anyone. Although Chivonne had come to the place where she was done with meeting guys with no real potential, she also realized that she wasn't getting any younger. She was always very shy and never bold enough to approach a man, and felt like it was completely unorthodox for her to make the first move and pursue a guy she liked.

Chivonne had been on several blind dates, a handful of "hook me up with your girl" dates and a few "he's nice…for someone else" dates. She spent many Saturday nights wishing she had just stayed in for the night instead of sitting at the dinner table, across from yet another guy who was either too short, too corny, or whom she did not find the least bit attractive. They were all nice guys and potential husband material, but they just were not quite what she was looking for.

She reminisced on one of the last dates she went on when she was in Philly, which turned her off from the dating scene for a couple months. It started off on a good note, as dates often did, but soon took a sharp turn for the worse.

He came into the office where she worked, as a client of the marketing firm she worked for. Well-mannered and friendly, he introduced himself. A week later, he called into her office, holding small talk, eventually getting around to the reason for his visit; to ask for her number and ask her out to lunch. In the days following, they chatted mostly through text messaging and a few phone conversations, quickly arranging a "pre-date", where they met at a local café, just to chat. That night, they decided to schedule a dinner date, where Mr. "Well-mannered" wasted no time in showing his true colors.

He picked her up from her house, and they rode to the restaurant together. On the way, he decided that he wanted to stop at the mall to pick up a pair of tennis shoes. Chivonne thought to herself, "No problem. The restaurant is just right by the mall, so it's no big deal." While he tried on the shoes he wanted to purchase, she sat quietly, and soon noticed that he began arguing with the saleswoman who was attending to the shoe department. "*I know this dude is not getting smart with her over some tennis shoes! It cannot possibly be that serious*," Chivonne thought to herself.

Listening a little more closely, Chivonne overheard him saying something about the saleswoman telling him that the shoe he wanted did not come in a certain color, but he had just so happened to find that color somewhere else on the sales floor. Whatever the situation was, Chivonne knew that it could not be worth an argument over shoe colors, when this guy was supposed to be on a date. It was then that she realized her first mistake. She wished in that moment, that she could get up from her seat, walk to her car, and drive away. It was too late.

"*Note to self*," she thought. "*Never allow a guy to pick me up for the first date. Always meet him there, just in case I need to flee the scene!*"

As if the department store fiasco was not enough to prove that this guy was not all that his text messages made him out to be, dinner sealed the deal. Mr. Well-mannered turned out to be not so well-mannered after all, getting into his second stand-off of the night, this time with their waitress. He seemed to have an issue with women whose job it was to help other people, which Chivonne found to be a major turn-off.

On the way home, Mr. Well-mannered drove his car as if he had never seen or heard of a speed limit, cutting someone off who had the right-of-way, almost getting hit on Chivonne's side of the car. To top off the night, he asked to borrow a couple of her movies that they had talked about earlier that night. In a desperate move to get rid of him as soon as possible, she ran inside, grabbed the movies, and said goodnight as she handed them over. She never saw or heard from him again.

2

Later that night

"Hey Chivonne!"

"Hey girl! Sorry I missed your call earlier. I had just gotten home from seeing my family off and had a million things in my hands. I couldn't get to my phone at the time."

"Oh, it's cool. I figured you were busy with work or something…as always."

"What's up?" Chivonne asked.

"I think I've found the perfect guy for you—"

"—Oh no! I'm not interested!" Chivonne yelled into the phone.

"Chivonne, seriously, I really think this guy could be the one! You know I just moved to a new office and I've met a few of my new co-workers, and there's this guy who is handsome, funny, and so down-to-earth, and I know for sure that he will be *your* guy. He's perfect!" Kye exclaimed, with more excitement than Chivonne cared to engage.

"Perfect?" Chivonne asked, her tone of voice proving that she was not at all interested in how *perfect* Kye claimed he was.

"Yes, *perfect!*"

"For *me?*"

"Yes, for *you!* Perfect for *you!* Trust me!"

"Kye, the last time I *trusted* you with setting me up on a date, I ended up sneaking out of the restaurant while he was in the men's room!"

"Hey, that was not my fault! I had just met that guy at a networking event for my job a few weeks before, and he seemed like a nice guy."

"Well, next time, assuming that I'll actually agree to a next time, I need you to do a little more pre-screening. If he didn't have to use the restroom, I would have had to pull a ninja escape to get out of there!"

"Chivonne, you are a beautiful and very successful woman, but you need a man!"

"And I am guessing that you believe that *this* man is the man I need?"

"Yes! But, *you'll* never know if you don't give him a chance to be that man."

As Kye continued, trying to convince Chivonne to give in and go on another blind date, Chivonne held a dialogue of her own.

"I'm not doing anything tomorrow night anyway, so why not go? Besides, this will be a chance for me to see more of the city, since I've been cramped up in my office and this apartment since I moved here. No! Wait! I promised myself that I would not go on anymore blind dates! I cannot do this to myself again. What if he is four feet tall? What if he has a gold tooth and an afro...and wears bell-bottomed pants and platforms with a goldfish in the heel? Okay. Really, Chivonne? Bell-bottomed pants? Does anyone still wear bell-bottomed pants? And why is he all of a sudden stuck in the seventies? Okay. Just breathe, Chivonne. Take a deep breath and relax. It's just a blind date. I am not traveling back in time. Besides, how will I ever meet anybody new if I only go to work, church, and the grocery store? I won't. That's how. Okay. I guess it will not kill me to give it just this last shot."

Chivonne finally gave in, giving Kye a chance at redemption from the debacle that was her last match-making effort.

"Oh, yaaay! I'm so glad you changed your mind, Chivonne. I promise you will not be disappointed in this one. I almost want to keep him for myself, but you know I have too much going on with the men in my life as it is."

Friday night came and it was not unlike every other Friday—busy and jam-packed with events—and Chivonne found the mere thought of getting dressed for a blind date to be more exhausting than it was worth. If this night were going to be like any other Friday night, it would either be a complete disaster or another disappointment that Chivonne was on yet another date with *someone else's* future husband.

After debating with herself about whether to go or not, she decided to renege, telling herself that she was, after all, *"a very busy woman with much better things to do than to meet a man by going on blind dates."* She knew there had to be a more practical way to meet the man God wanted her to marry. Using her busy work-life as an excuse for not stepping out of her comfort zone, she called Kye to break the news, reaching her voicemail instead.

"Hey Kye, I am not going to make it tonight because I am really exhausted from today and I honestly do not want to meet another man under five feet tall, so please let your co-worker know that I am very sorry for cancelling on such short notice, but I think I'm going to call it a night. You guys enjoy yourselves. Give me a call back when you get this message. Later!"

If Chivonne had been honest with herself, exhaustion was not what kept her from going on that date. "Why do I have to be *blind* to meet someone?" she joked to herself. "I have been going on blind date after blind date, and it's just tiring. I cannot do this again. There has to be a better way."

Chivonne quickly slipped into her pajamas, just in case she would be tempted to change her mind again. She popped her favorite movie, *Brown Sugar,* into the DVD player, yet again, and got ready for her weekend movie night ritual. Something about that movie reminded her that there had to be someone out there who loved her just like Dre loved Sydney. And even though she had watched it a thousand times before, and could quote the script as if she wrote it herself, each time she watched it was just as dreamy as the first time she saw it.

"When did you fall in love with Hip Hop?" she thought to herself. "Ha! Better yet, when *will* I fall in love with Hip Hop? None of these guys I've come in contact with have even come close to that feeling. That childhood crush, real love feeling. That *'I got your back, no matter what'* feeling. Not even close. But, I'm not going to lose hope. I know God will send him…one day. And one day I'll have a Dre of my very own and he'll tell me, *'you're the perfect verse over a tight beat.'* One day soon, I hope."

With popcorn popping in the microwave, Chivonne laid down to take a quick nap before starting the movie. Before she knew it, she was waking up the next morning to the warmth of the sun shining through her bedroom window, realizing that she never even got around to watching the movie.

Her phone vibrated. She picked up the phone from the nightstand beside her bed, expecting to see a missed call from Kye, but it was a text message from one of her childhood friends, Trey, who had moved to LA a year before she did.

"Yo!"

"Yo!"

"How was your date last night?"

"I didn't go."

"Figures. What are you doing?"

"Um. Just woke up. I'm about to go to the market and pick up a few things…probably grab lunch."

"Cool. I'll be there in 25 min. That

should be enough time for you to get ready. And make sure you brush your teeth, too. I can smell your morning breath through this text message!"

"Very funny! I'll make sure my breath and underarms are extra funky in your car because YOU, my friend, are driving since you have all of the jokes this morning."

"LOL! Fair enough. OMW."

Trey arrived in precisely twenty-five minutes. The perfectionist that he was, he was always on time. Unlike Trey, Chivonne was a spontaneous type of girl, which is why they could never date. The thought of them eventually ending up together had undoubtedly crossed her mind a few times, but his friendship outweighed the risk of losing him to a bad breakup.

Chivonne grew up in the church, and since meeting a guy in college did not pan out, she hoped that after college she would meet her future husband in ministry. She wanted to be able to tell the same story that she had heard from so many other women, that she was "minding her business, serving the Lord," and "he just came out of nowhere and snatched me up," much like her grandmother's story. As great of a story as it would be to tell, she had lost hope of it ever being *her* story. Although she had met a handful of young men who also served in ministry, none of them even came close to the type of man she had always wanted to grow old with. She had imagined herself with someone who had a heart of gold and the body of an NBA star. As far-fetched as it seemed to her, she still wanted that tall, lean, and chiseled frame of a man, who was also a gentleman, a family man, and her best friend.

Just like every other single woman, she had her list. Full of details like "tall, about 6'4, caramel complexion with a drop of chocolate, financially independent, funny, no earrings, no tattoos, outgoing, intelligent, *saved, sanctified and filled with the Holy Ghost,*" the list went on. She made sure to cover every one of her bases.

Chivonne was often told that she would never find a man who would meet all of the requirements on her list, but she was determined to find the man of her dreams, or at least let God know what type of man to send her, as if God needed any help.

After sitting in an hour of LA traffic, Chivonne and Trey finally made it to the market to browse around and catch each other up on recent happenings. They grabbed lunch at *The Creole Kitchen*, Chivonne's favorite New Orleans style restaurant, and bought a couple bags of fresh produce. That was always her favorite part. Visiting the market on the weekends reminded her of the times that her grandmother would take her to the farmer's market on Saturday mornings, to pick up fresh ingredients for Sunday dinner. Although she missed those times in Philly, she was happy to be on her own in LA, to start a few Saturday morning traditions of her own.

Trey wanted to stop by *Casual Male*, the men's clothing store, before they headed home. Ironically, Chivonne hated shopping, but Trey loved it. Because he was a *shop-o-holic*, or so Chivonne would say, she knew he would be in the clothing store for quite some time. Foregoing the opportunity to follow Trey around the store, she opted to sit outside on the bench and wait for him, pulling out her cell phone to pass the time. As she was going through her phone and catching up on her social media feeds, she noticed a caramel complexion, lean-framed handsome man towering over everyone he passed, walking into the store where Trey happened to be shopping. The usual self-pep talk came right on queue.

"Hmmm. He sure is cute. He's tall…he's got to be at least 6'4! Casually dressed, clean-cut, athletic build, and confident looking, just how I like them. Hmmm…no! Stop it Chivonne! Just stop. That man is not thinking about you and as fine as he is, he is probably married already. But, I can just go into the store and look at him. There is no harm in that, right? Yeah, I'll just go inside and pretend to look for Trey, and if I just so happen to glance at him, then it is what it is. Wait! If I go inside, he may see me actually talking to Trey and he'll think we are together. I certainly do not want him to think that I am not single. Okay, never mind. Just forget it. I am not going in there because I do not want to appear desperate. I do not want him to think that I

am with Trey and, besides, I don't even want to think about men right now. I need to 'focus on God and not on finding a man' (mocking the singleness self-help books she often read). Okay. Not going in. I'm going to sit right here and scroll through these tweets and behave as if I never saw him. As a matter of fact, let me open up this Bible app, so I can keep my mind stayed on God!"

"Chi, guess who I saw inside shopping!" Trey yelled from behind as he walked towards her. "Chi" was a nickname Trey gave her when they were just kids—he thought it suited her well since she was always really *shy.*

"Who?" she asked.

"Marcus, my homeboy who owns the barbershop next door to your store! You two went out, didn't you?"

"Yeah, we did...I guess."

"You guess?" Trey asked.

"Yeah, we went out once and he stopped coming by the store after that night. I guess that meant our date didn't go too well," she said, sarcastically. "Anyway, are you ready to go? I need to get out of here, quickly! And speaking of which, can we stop by my boutique? I need to pick up some paperwork that I need to work on before the concert tonight."

"Okay..." Trey said, looking perplexed. "What just happened...and what concert?" he asked, with his usual facial expression that was a mixture of confusion and guilt.

"The concert at *The Ville* that I told you about three weeks ago and you said you would go with me."

"Um. Oh, *that* concert. Yeah. I sort of forgot about that and made plans for tonight," he mumbled, reluctantly. "I have...a date."

"A *what?*"

"A date."

"With *who?*"

"A *woman.*"

"*What* woman? Who in their right mind has agreed to be seen with you in public?"

"Well, you, for one, since you are standing here. And secondly, I met her last weekend on my flight home. We chatted the whole ride and exchanged numbers once we landed. We've talked on the phone every day since. I really think this girl might be the one, Chi!"

"Oh, *really?*" Chivonne said, raising her eyebrows, surprised that Trey would even utter those words.

"Yes, *really.* And why are you so surprised? We are not getting any younger, you know…emphasis on *we.* We're in our thirties now and before we know it, we'll be forty. It's about time you settled down yourself."

"Settle down, Trey? As if I have been roaming the streets aimlessly, gallivanting with every man with legs that crosses my path. Trust me, I am ready for my knight in shining armor when he comes along, but I am not looking for him. I am waiting for my husband to find me, emphasis on *waiting for him to find me.* When the right man comes along, then I'll be ready, but I am not out here looking for him. I'm not desperate. And, by the way, I am only thirty and I am so surprised because not too long ago you were talking about how much you didn't want to get married and that you'll be a bachelor for the rest of your life. Remember that?" Chivonne asked him.

"Okay. I hear you, Chi, but you have to put yourself out there. Get out and mingle! Talk to people that you don't know. Do things you would not usually do. You have to spread your wings, little birdie!"

"Trey, my dear friend, I am all for socializing and mingling, but I believe that God will send my husband to me in my environment because it will be *his* environment, too. I don't think that I have to start doing things outside of my element in order to find a husband. I'm not going to start turning up every weekend in order to be found!"

"You could be right, but where has that gotten you so far?" he asked, hesitantly, to not offend her. "Anyway, we've got to get going because I need all the time I can get to be fresh for my date tonight."

"Oh, excuse me, Mr. Makes-plans-with-best-friend-and-forgets-about-said-plans-when-a-pretty-girl-comes-along. And if you need *that* much time to get ready, maybe you are not so fresh after all."

"Don't be like that, Chi."

"Enjoy your date, Trey. I hope she doesn't like you!" she scoffed.

"Really, Chi?!" Trey replied. "You don't mean that."

"Of course I don't but I was really hoping you'd tag along to the concert since I don't have anyone else to go with."

"What about your neighbor, Kye? She's into that kind of thing, right?" he asked.

"Yeah, she is, but she's probably out somewhere match-making two random people off of the street as we speak! I'll just have to mosey on down by myself. And you know what? I am going to do just that, and have the TIME-OF-MY-LIFE-WITH-OUT-YOU!" she exclaimed, pointing her index finger at him with each word, making sure he heard every word she said.

"I love you, my beautiful, forgiving, and understanding best friend," Trey said, grinning from ear to ear, squeezing Chivonne's arms in a plea for her forgiveness.

"Where did you park?" Chivonne uttered, while freeing herself from his grasp, turning away and walking ahead of him.

"Not exactly sure, and I'm not so sure why we parked so far away! I guess I just pulled into the first space I saw," Trey replied. "Oh, wait! It's right here," he said, pointing to the car to his left.

"We almost walked right past it!" Chivonne laughed. "You're not going to open my car door for me, Trey?" she asked, as she walked towards the passenger side door, her eyes following him as he walked straight to the driver's side door. "I've got to train you for your date tonight! You're not ready!"

"Ha ha! You might be right! And, as fine as she is, I definitely need to be ready. Your boy has got to be *New Husband of the Year* soon, Chi!" Trey bellowed, as he skipped to the other side of the car to open the door for Chivonne. "And I have to remember to pull her chair out and wait for her to sit down before I do. That's the one I always forget!" he added, closing the door after her legs were in.

"Yes, absolutely. Remember to let her order first and do not let her pay for dinner! I hear a lot of women are doing that now. I guess it's the whole 'I've got my own money' movement. I'm a little old school, because I still expect the man to pay for the first date, but if she's one of those new women, she may offer to pay. Don't let her. You will never make it to a second date, I assure you!"

On the ride back to Chivonne's place, she let him in on all of the old school first date rules and how he should be a perfect gentleman, not just for the first date, but for the long haul.

After schooling Trey on what to do and what not to do on his date, Chivonne shared with Trey the reason why she decided not to go on the blind the night before.

"Trey, I have just had enough of being the victim of Kye's match-making," she began. "I've given up on trying so hard. I just want to meet a man naturally, not by force."

"I can understand that, but there are a lot of people who are hooked up these days. Some people even find their spouses online! I couldn't do it, but I hear a lot of people are doing that," Trey replied.

"Yeah, I've heard that too, but that's just not for me! I would be terrified to even talk to, much less meet in person someone I met on the internet! That's outrageous!" she responded, as Trey pulled into a parking spot in front of her apartment building. "Okay, well, I will talk to you later. And I'll be sure to rub in what you missed at the concert."

"Later, Chi," Trey answered, giving her a side-eye mixed with a bit of shame.

As Chivonne walked inside and pulled her phone out of her purse, she realized she had a missed call and text message from Kye. She opted to read the text over calling her back right away.

"Hey Chivonne. I got your message last night. I'm sorry you couldn't make it. My co-worker says he is sorry he did not get the chance to meet the beautiful girl I told him about, and he hopes that you can reschedule for another time when you're available. TTYL."

3

The last thing Chivonne wanted was to go to the concert alone, but since her *ex-best friend* ditched her for his date, she decided to go alone, in lieu of asking someone else to join her at the last minute. Since moving across the country with no family and little to no friends, Chivonne had mastered the art of *going alone.*

After searching her closets and dresser drawers for over an hour, trying on what seemed like every piece of clothing she owned, she finally pieced together what she thought was the cutest outfit that she could. She preferred to keep it classy when it came to fashion, and she always kept her hair and makeup simple, yet elegant.

With everything going on at the boutique lately, free time like she had that night did not come too often, so she set out to have a great time, even if it were with herself. Once she arrived, she made her way inside and began to scan the room for someone—anyone—that she may know.

"She looks familiar...but, she's with a guy, so I'll pass on that. Don't want to be a third wheel. Hey, I think he goes to my church, and he's alone, but I don't want him to think I am trying to holler, so...no. Hmmm. That guy looks nice. Oh wait...he is probably with that woman hanging on his arm. Pass."

After another quick scan, she noticed another young lady who she recognized from the church she had been attending, who also appeared to be going solo that night. Without hesitation, Chivonne walked over to her, quickly sparking up a conversation.

"Hey...Jennifer, right?"

"Yes! I thought you looked like someone I know! And you

actually remember my name! You attend Faith Church, right?"

"Yeah, I do. And I'm pretty good with names. I'm Chivonne," extending her hand.

"Oh, you're much better than me! I cannot remember anyone's name to save my life. Good to see you, Chivonne!"

"You too! You picked a pretty good spot," Chivonne said, looking around. "What time did you get here?"

"Just a few minutes ago. I got here early to get a good spot because my cousin likes to stand in the back. He'll probably be the tallest person here once he gets here. Leave it to him, and I won't see a thing! Oh, there he is," waving to get his attention.

Chivonne turned around. *"Oh my gosh! That's the guy I saw at the market!"* she said to herself. *"This cannot be real. Somebody pinch me because I have to be dreaming. Okay. Just chill, Chivonne. You still do not even know if this guy is single, or if he will even be interested in you at all. Chill."*

"Hey Chase, this is Chivonne. She goes to our church."

"Hi Chivonne, pleasure to meet you," extending his hand and looking at her with the slightest smile. "Hey Jennifer," he said, hugging her.

"Good to meet you, too, Chase. The pleasure is *all* mine."

Chivonne was usually very shy and never good at flirting, but that night was different. She wasn't completely sure, but she felt like Chase was also doing a little bit of flirting with her. After he flashed what seemed to her like an inviting and unassuming smile, Chivonne offered her giddy chuckle in response to every one of his jokes, quickly becoming comfortable with him. In fact, they picked up conversation so well that Chase's cousin had to remind him that she was still standing there.

They continued to chat until Chivonne slipped away to use the ladies' room before the concert began. Feeling like the third wheel, Jennifer took that opportunity to add her own two cents.

"What was *that*?" Jennifer asked Chase.

"What was *what*?" Chase asked, pretending to not know what she was asking about.

"*That*," motioning back and forth between Chase and the bathroom where Chivonne was. "You and Chivonne. The match made in heaven that was just made manifest here on earth! What just happened?"

"She's nice. Uh, *really* nice. And she's cute. Beautiful, actually."

"Yeah, you are just the man, aren't you? Blind date last night and making love connections tonight. You've changed, Chase! You used to be so shy around women and now you're booking the ladies like you've been doing it for years!"

"Uh...I haven't booked her...yet. And about that blind date...it didn't happen. She cancelled. But this girl..."

"This girl what?" she asked, eagerly.

"I'm kind of speechless, actually," Chase responded. "You know how difficult it is to meet someone you click with right away!"

"The minister is speechless? Wow! This is getting good! Well, Miss What's-her-face missed out last night, but lucky for you, there is a ram in the bush!"

"Right! That was her loss, but I am not even worried about that. My co-worker never even told me her name."

"Oh, here she comes! Act natural," Jennifer whispered.
The concert began as Chivonne walked back to where Jennifer and Chase were standing. During the concert, Chivonne had every thought about Chase racing through her mind that she could barely

enjoy the music.

In such a short time, Chivonne could tell that Chase was friendly, well-spoken, and humble, not to mention he was the perfect height. She knew she was attracted to him, but she did not want to jump ahead and assume that he had the same thoughts about her. She did everything she could to keep from thinking about him, considering how good he smelled standing next to her.

"Oh my goodness, he smells so good! He must have jumped out of the shower and came straight here! He smells like fresh linen and some expensive name brand cologne. And it's not too much, thank the Lord, but it's just enough! It's subtle enough so that I don't smell him from across the room, but I get a good whiff standing close enough. Maybe I shouldn't be standing so close to him! Am I standing too close? Well, if I were, he would have moved, but he hasn't moved so I guess he doesn't mind. Or maybe I should just pay attention to this concert that I spent my money on and drove all the way out here for! Yeah, that sounds like a good idea, Chivonne. Lord have mercy on my soul! Forgive me, Lord, for I know exactly what I'm doing! He smells divine! Pay attention!"

Throughout the concert, there wasn't much time to chat aside from general concert small-talk like, "have you seen these guys in concert before?" or "how often do you attend events like this?" When the concert came to an end, Chase's cousin pulled him aside, as inconspicuously as possible, as the three of them walked together toward the exit.

"So, you like her, huh?" Jennifer whispered, with a huge grin on her face.

"She's nice," he answered, quietly and quickly, without looking down at her, as to not let Chivonne know that he was talking about her.

"*Nice*, Chase?" Jennifer asked. "Just *nice*? The way you were beaming like a light saber an hour ago and forgot about your dear old cousin who invited you to this concert, she's *just* nice?" raising her voice a little.

"Why are you so loud?! She *is* standing right there," Chase whispered, with his teeth clinched together, his lips barely moving.

"Whatever, Chase. It's no secret that you're attracted to her. It's all over your face. I know you! You ain't fooling me! And I'm pretty sure she kind of likes you a little bit, too, the way she lit up when you walked up on us, and how she was standing so close to you the whole night. She is definitely felling you, for sure!"

"Oh, stop it! You're reading into this way too much." Although Chase did not want to admit it, he had wanted Chivonne to be interested in him, and he wanted everything his cousin said to be true. "And besides, she was not standing too close to me, and even if she were, it wouldn't have been such a bad thing."

"Mmm hmm. Even though you won't admit it, Chase, I can see in your starry eyes that you're feeling her! I'm gonna disappear and let you do your thing. Make sure you *get those digits*! Make our family proud!"

"No one says 'get those digits' anymore, Jen. You need to say goodbye to the nineties!" Chase joked.

"Chase, you know I'm only kidding and you know exactly what I mean! I still love you, though!"

While Chase and his cousin whispered to each other, Chivonne walked slowly behind him, pulling out her phone to text Trey, rubbing in to him how he missed such a great concert, and to inquire about his date.

Keeping her eye on Chase and his cousin, she thought to herself, *"Should I hang around and see if he wants to chat or should I just leave? I know I look really strange right now, walking behind them, but I don't want to just walk away without saying anything. Well, maybe he isn't thinking about me since he hasn't turned around to say anything. He probably doesn't even notice that I'm behind them. Just leave, Chivonne!"* Just before she walked away, Chase and Jennifer turned around.

"Hey, I was wondering what happened to you," Jennifer said,

pretending to not have noticed Chivonne behind them. Chase stepped aside to answer his phone. "It was really great to see you again and enjoy the concert with you and my *handsome* cousin," winking at Chase. He continued on his call, flashing an innocent smile, quickly looking away to hide his blushing. "Hopefully, I will see you at church in the morning."

"Yes! Same here. It was great seeing you, too. I see you around church often, so it was nice to see a familiar face tonight!" Chivonne replied. Chase stood by as his phone conversation ended. "I'll be at church bright and early in the morning."

"Okay, have a good night!" Jennifer answered, as she walked away. "Bye Chase!"

"Don't mind my cousin," Chase said, walking toward Chivonne. "She's always joking around. I can't take her anywhere! Anyway, can I walk you to your car?"

"Sure," she answered, relieved that Chase made the first move and impressed that he asked.

As Chivonne began walking to her car, Chase following, she went on and on about the concert and how she was a huge fan of the group who performed. As she was talking, she could not help but to notice Chase's undivided attention to her; something she had never experienced before. The fact that he seemed to hang onto her every word made her feel unusually comfortable talking to him, unlike any guy she had met before. It was as if she was breathing fresh air for the first time in a long time. She never wanted the night to end.

"So, I take it you *really* enjoyed the concert?" Chase asked jokingly.

"Yes!" she laughed, "I did! I haven't seen them in concert since I left Philadelphia. I was so excited when I found out that they would be in town this weekend."

"Oh, so you're an East Coast girl! How long have you been in

LA?"

"Just a few months. I visited once, before I decided to move, and immediately fell in love. I knew it was only a matter of time before I was back for good."

"Yeah, LA has a way of making people immediately fall in love," Chase replied, looking away after realizing the awkward moment he had created. They both smiled, intentionally avoiding eye contact.

"I wouldn't dream of moving across the country like that. You're very brave," Chase continued.

"Well, it was one of those decisions that I had to make if I ever wanted to realize all the dreams I have. God certainly orchestrated everything because if He hadn't, I probably would have never made it over here. I'd still be stuck in Philly, wishing I had taken that leap of faith."

"Oh, absolutely! Once you let go of fear and allow God to show you His plan for you, He will give you the grace to do what you never could have done on your own."

"Yes, sir. You're so right!" she exclaimed.

"Sir? That makes me feel old!" he laughed.

"Oh, I call every man sir. It's just my way of saying buddy."

They both laughed.

"It's getting late, but…I'd really like to continue this conversation," Chase said cautiously, trying to gauge Chivonne's interest.

Taken completely off guard, she was speechless.

"So, would you like to have coffee sometime, ma'am?" Chase asked. "Maybe a spot of tea?" he added, with a British accent.

"Sure, that would be cool," laughing at his accent.

"Okay, cool. Let's exchange numbers and I'll give you a call to set up a date. Sounds good?"

"Sounds good."

As Chivonne unlocked her doors with her key fob, Chase walked over to open her door.

"Let me get that for you," Chase proposed.

"Well, aren't you just the perfect gentleman! Thank you. I appreciate that," she replied, as she got into her car.

"No problem at all. My parents taught me well!" he responded. "Enjoy the rest of your evening, Chivonne."

"You, too, Chase. Goodnight." Chase closed her car door after her feet were in.

On the long ride home, Chivonne's first thought was to call her older sister, Blair, to tell her all about the guy she just met, but she did not want to jump to conclusions like she had done in the past and she did not want to wake her up in the middle of the night since she was in a different time zone.

Chivonne had a really bad habit of playing out potential situations in her head, becoming disappointed when things did not work out exactly the way she had imagined they would. Reminiscing on past dates and what were *almost* relationships, she remembered the guy from the neighborhood that she grew up in, that never quite happened. From a very young age, he was in love with her, but far too immature for her to take him seriously.

She thought about the guy she almost dated in high school that cheated on her before they were even exclusive. *"That was a huge mistake ever giving him the time of day! I still cannot believe he did that! And I really liked him,"* she thought.

She couldn't forget about the one who had an attitude with the waitress on their first date, and borrowed her movies, knowing he had no intention on bringing them back to her. *"I couldn't care any less whether or not I saw him again, but man, I wanted my movies back!"*

From the guy who seemed perfect in the beginning, but she knew he wasn't the one, to the one who was a nice guy, but she just was not attracted to him, none of those *almost* relationships ever seemed to work out. And what was most frustrating to Chivonne was that she somehow seemed to long after the ones who were not at all interested in her, or so it seemed, and she ended up on dates with all of the guys that she did not see as worthy of her time. None of these relationships, or *would-be* relationships, ever worked out and she was tired of trying. She had given up all hope of ever meeting a guy that she actually liked and who actually liked her, and was decent enough to spend any amount of time with.

Even through remembering so much disappointment in her past encounters, somehow Chivonne knew that this time would be different, because Chase was different. He was a breath of fresh air.

She finally made it home and headed straight for the shower. Putting on some music, she tried to take her mind off of Chase and drown out the thoughts of what *could be.*

"Okay. So, I am not going to jump to conclusions because I'm just not going down that road. I don't even want to think about him!" coaching herself to approach this situation differently this time around. *"I don't want to make up some fairytale about how we will fall in love with each other and have a million babies and travel the world. I'm not doing that this time around. My focus is on other things that are more important to me. And besides, he only asked for a coffee date. I don't even know if I like him for real! He might turn out to be a jerk or already have a million babies! Okay. Stop that, too, Chivonne. Don't prepare yourself for a bad situation just because all the others didn't work out. Be open. Yes! That's what I'll do. I'll be open to whatever happens, but I'm not looking for anything special."*

With a mountain of thoughts and doubts to overcome, Chivonne drilled herself to look at the reality of things, being careful to not tear down what had not yet been built. She got dressed for bed after her shower and realized she had a missed call on her cell phone.

"I bet it's Trey calling to tell me how bad his date turned out and to apologize for ditching me," she said to herself. She opened the missed call and saw that it was Chase who had called a few minutes before, but he hadn't left a voicemail message. *"Wow, so much for the three-day rule! Should I call him back?"* she thought. *"Maybe he mistakenly called me or butt-dialed me. No. I'm not calling him back. That would seem desperate, and I am definitely not desperate. I'm focusing on God and not on finding a man!"*

The phone rang again. She held the phone in her hand, staring at Chase's name as it lit up the screen.

She answered. "Hello?"

"Hey Chivonne. It's Chase. Did I wake you?"

"No, I'm not in bed yet. Just getting ready for church tomorrow."

"Oh." He paused. "I know it is really kind of bizarre for me to be calling you at this hour, especially since we just met a few hours ago, but I felt like I wanted to completely destroy the three-day rule and call you right away!"

"Ha! Yes, you certainly exterminated the rule and created a new three-*hour* rule," she laughed. "It's no problem. What's up? How was your ride home?" she asked.

"It was good. You know, the usual scenic route from that side of town to where I live is always exciting, with all the buildings and streets and trees and cars," Chase said, sarcastically. "Anyway, I really enjoyed meeting you tonight. And the concert wasn't bad either."

"Absolutely! I enjoyed meeting and briefly getting to know you as well. I wish we could have chatted a little longer, but it was getting late."

"Yeah, I wouldn't want you turning into a pumpkin out there!"

Chivonne giggled.

"So, let's get the inevitable small talk out of the way, so we can get down to the nitty gritty!"

"O...k," Chivonne said, cautiously.

"How old are you? What do you do for fun? What's your favorite color? Do you have any siblings? Where did you go to college? What's your five-year plan? What's your credit score? How many kids do you want? What's your blood type?" Chase lightheartedly shot off a series of questions, one after the other, not expecting Chivonne to remember every question, much less answer any of them honestly.

"Ummm...30. Anything that's fun. Don't have a favorite color. One sister. Penn State. Marriage, kids, and business growth. 775. Five boys. And I don't know my blood type. And you?" Chivonne answered each question just as quickly has Chase had asked them. She did not miss a beat.

"Wow, you're good! And you keep up. Well, I'm 37. I like long walks on the beach. You know...the usual," Chase said, in jest. "Favorite color is green. I have two sisters and one brother. I'm the oldest. I went to UCLA. Marriage, kids, and ministry growth. Credit not as good as yours, so, I'm too embarrassed to say! And I want as many kids as my future wife can birth. Why only boys? And why so many?" Chase inquired.

"Wow! You have a pretty big family compared to mine. I can only imagine the fun times you guys had growing up in that house. For me, growing up with just an older sister sometimes had me wondering what it would be like to have a brother, and once my sister left for college, I was pretty much on my own. So, I've always imagined myself with a big family of my own. And quite honestly, I think it would be best that I'm the only woman in the house! And you didn't tell me your blood type, Chase."

"Ha! Yes, I totally forgot that! I actually don't know mine either so I guess I shouldn't have asked you! But, yes, there were lots of fun times and some hard times. And sometimes I wished I was an only child."

"I can see how that could happen. Sometimes in the midst of all the chaos, you just want to be alone, but it's kind of difficult to be alone, with three other siblings."

Chivonne and Chase more than hit it off that night. Their conversation lasted about seven hours, well into the next morning. They talked about everything from past birthday parties, worst Christmas gifts, and crazy school pictures, to prayer, reaching for goals, and everything in between. Chase had to be up in three hours to get ready for church, where he taught Sunday school, so they were forced to end their phone conversation around 5:00 AM.

What Chivonne learned about Chase in a matter of hours was more than she had ever learned about all of the guys she dated, combined. Chase seemed to be open to sharing much more about his life than most guys she had met. More importantly, Chase was more open to learning about her life than most guys were. He was interested in *her*.

4

April 15

"Minister Chase, a moment of your time?"

"Absolutely. How are you, Pastor Young?"

"Doing well. I wanted to just thank you again for taking on the task of teaching Sunday school. You know the kids really love you! In all my years of ministry, I've never seen so many kids so excited for Sunday school. If I didn't know any better, I'd think you were giving away free food every Sunday!"

"Ha! No, I'm not giving away free food. I just love teaching those kids and seeing their lives changed each week. It's a reward for me, actually! And, you know Chase love the kids!"

"And the kids love Chase, so I hear! I've even had some of the parents tell me how much they appreciate that their kids have someone closer to their age to listen to them and answer their questions on a level that they can understand. They've been able to understand what you've taught them, even at such a young age. It's pretty awesome, Chase! I am really honored and grateful that you are doing this. I cannot thank you enough."

"It's absolutely no problem at all, Pastor Young. You know I have the greatest respect for you and would do anything that you believe God wants me to do for this ministry, so thank you for trusting me and allowing me to teach them."

"You have a heart of gold, Chase! Truly a great man of God."

"Thank you, Pastor. That means a lot."

"You're welcome, and I won't hold you any longer. Enjoy the

rest of this beautiful Sunday afternoon."

"You too."

On the way to his car, Chase pulled out his cell phone and noticed a text message from Chivonne.

"Good morning Sunshine! Thanks for making me miss church this morning. LOL! I enjoyed getting to know you last night/this morning. Talk to you soon!"

Chase smiled from ear to ear as he carefully crafted his reply.

"Good morning to you, Chivonne! I guess I will take the blame this time for keeping you up all night, but who's to blame for keeping ME up all night?"

"I'll take that. ☺"

"What are you up to today?"

"Not much. I just woke up not too long ago."

"Hungry?"

"How did you know?"

"☺ I think I got to know you pretty well last night! Meet me at The Oak Diner in an hour?"

"OK. I think I know where that is. I'll be there!"

Completely engrossed in his reply, Chase was caught off guard when Jennifer yelled his name, as if she were not standing right next to him the entire time.

"Chase!" she shouted. Peeping over his shoulder to see the screen on his phone. "Whose text message has you grinning from ear to ear, over here boo lovin' right after church, still on the church grounds?"

"Chivonne's text message, since you're so nosey all of a sudden!" he answered.

"Chivonne? You mean the girl you met last night? The one you've known for less than twenty-four hours? When did *that* happen?"

"Uh…last night after the concert…after you left and told me to 'get those digits'," Chase mocked, holding up air quotes.

"Oh, you didn't waste any time! You are just a smooth operator, aren't you?" Jennifer asked, jokingly. "So when are you going to call her? When are you going to ask her out on a *daaaaate*?" she teased, playfully poking him in his arm.

He snared at her as he made brunch plans with Chivonne. "Actually, we spoke on the phone last night for several hours, and I'm blissfully exhausted right now."

"What? Last night? I guess it's true what they say. He who findeth a wife, findeth a *good thang*."

"Oh, so all of a sudden you're a Bible scholar, huh? And who said anything about findeth-ing a wife?" Chase said, mocking her.

"Well, she must be a *good thang* if you had to move so quickly! And yes, I am a Bible scholar, as a matter of fact! Don't play me, Chase! I was quoting scripture from the good book way before you even stepped foot in a church pulpit."

"Anyway, I'm meeting this *good thang*, as you would say, for brunch in an hour, so I've got to go. I'll see you tonight at my mom's birthday dinner."

"Seven PM sharp!" Jennifer shouted, as she walked away.

Chase never would have admitted to his cousin at that moment, but he did actually believe that Chivonne could be the woman he would spend the rest of his life with. Although he had just met her the night before, he knew he absolutely wanted for her to be his good thing, and he hoped that that was where God was leading him.

Chivonne met Chase at his favorite restaurant that served all his favorites like pancakes, waffles, crepes, French toast, home fries, scrambled eggs, grits, oatmeal, and omelets. After stuffing themselves until they could not take another bite, Chase dropped a bomb.

"Chivonne, I want to tell you something," he began.

"Okay. What's going on?" she asked, the look of concern all over her face.

"I was engaged to be married three months ago."

"O…K. What happened that you are *not* married?" she asked, almost unwillingly.

"I called it off."

"Why? What happened?" she asked.

"A lot happened. To start, I'm not sure if you want to know *everything*, but I just feel like you should at least know about it."

"Chase, I'm here," she said, looking directly into his eyes. "If I didn't want to know anything about you, trust me, I would not be here."

"Well, that's good to know!" he smiled. "I'm honored that you're here and that you're interested. And I really want to be completely honest and tell you that I'm very interested in you and who you are and what you like. I want to know everything about you." Chivonne began to blush. "Now, I'm hoping that knowing that I've been engaged before doesn't change what you think of me, whatever that is. But, I would like to pursue a friendship and possibly something more with you, so I really want to start off on the right foot and be honest about who I am."

"It doesn't change what I think about you, Chase. We've all been through things in our lives, and you and I just met, so I can't expect you to be perfect or anything. I'd be naïve to think that you wouldn't have a past." Although Chivonne was a bit surprised to hear about Chase's previous engagement, she was careful not to immediately write him off.

Relieved at what she said, Chase took a deep breath before responding.

"Yeah! Breathe, Chase!" Chivonne continued. "It's absolutely okay to have a past. I get that. I get that things happen. I get that things do not always turn out the way we want them to or go the way they even appeared to be going, but that's life, Chase. You don't have to be ashamed of what you've been through. Look at it this way. If you had not had that experience and gone through what was probably a bad breakup, with lots of crying and arguing and money wasted, you would not be the man you are today and you would not be sitting here with me today."

"Now that is something to be thankful for! I would not be sitting across from one of the most beautiful women I've ever met. That is something to thank God for!"

Chivonne blushed. "Thank you, Chase. You are not half bad yourself!" she said, avoiding eye contact with him to keep form blushing further.

"Let's get out of here before they kick us out for holding up a table!" Chase exclaimed.

"Yeah, we do not want to get kicked out because I definitely want to come back. I really like this place!" Chivonne replied, as they stood up from the table and walked toward the exit. Chase held his smile. "What?" she asked, looking back at him as he held the door for her.

"Nothing," he answered, smiling. "I'm glad you like this place." Chase was happy to know that Chivonne loved his favorite restaurant because his ex-fiancé hated it. "I want to show you something," he said.

"Show me what?" she asked.

"Just follow me."

Chase took Chivonne to one of his favorite past-times, a quiet park near the house he grew up in. As a teenager, Chase would spend hours there alone, daydreaming of his future. As an adult, that park became his favorite place to pray, whenever he needed time alone to sort out his thoughts. It was there that Chase heard from God about being a minister. It was there that God showed Chase his purpose and how he would fulfill it. And it was there that he also came to the realization that he needed to end his relationship with his ex-fiancé. He loved that he could go to that place to get away from his daily routine and be alone with God. He felt the need to share this with Chivonne—something he never shared with anyone else before.

"So what made this park so special to you as a kid?" Chivonne inquired.

"Well, my parents bought the house right after I was born and my mother said she would bring me here when I was a baby. Of course, I was too young at the time to remember that far back, but once she went back to work after having me, she would bring me here on the weekends, to play. Since none of my siblings were born yet, it was just us two. I have so many memories of her and I just walking on the trail or having a bag lunch on the grass over there, once I was a little older," Chase said, pointing to an open patch of ground that had more dirt than grass. "And I can remember one of the times we came here was right before she had my sister. She brought me out here to tell me that I was going to be a big brother and she wanted me to know that she would still love and care for me just as much, once the baby came, but that she might have to pay a little more attention to the new addition to the family. She told me that it was going to be my responsibility to make sure that my sister was taken care of and that she was safe whenever my parents were not around. So, I've been coming here for years. Whenever I need to pray without being distracted, this is the first place I come to."

Chivonne was quiet. She had found a somewhat clean, but dusty spot on the ground to sit on. Looking into the bare, leafless trees, she held onto everything Chase had said. As he explained to her how he became a better man every time he visited that park, she, too, had found solace there, in that moment. For once, since moving to LA, she was in a place where she felt like her eyes were finally open to see whatever God wanted to show her and her heart was ready to receive all that God had planned for her life.

"When I started dating my ex, I had stopped coming here," Chase continued. "I tried to bring her here once, but she hated the outdoors, so, of course that did not go too well."

"What happened?" Chivonne asked.

"What happened that day or what happened with her?" Chase asked.

"Either one, I guess. Whatever you feel comfortable telling me."

"Well, that day, she had gotten eaten by about twenty mosquitos, and it rained, and…well, it was just awful for her. I thought it was pretty funny, so of course, she scolded me for that."

"And with her?" Chivonne asked.

"To make a *very* long story short, she was not who I needed. She wasn't someone I could see myself being with five years from now, much less forever. She hated the fact that I spend a lot of time mentoring and teaching kids, because that means less time with her. But, to be honest with you, I enjoyed my time away from her more than the time that I was with her! We got along okay, but it just was not the right fit. To the naked eye, and in my mother's eyes, she was the one. But, in my heart and because of where I know I'm going in life, she wouldn't fit. And, well, she ended up moving back to her hometown in Texas a couple weeks after we broke up. She said something about having a job lined up and planning to move anyway."

"Wow! That's kind of crazy, Chase! Just like that, she up and left?"

"Yup, just like that."

"Have you spoken to her since then?" she asked.

"Not really. She sent me an email once she got there to tell me she made it down okay and was *doing just fine without me,*" Chase said, with air quotes. "I replied and told her I was happy for her, which I really am, and that I was glad she made it safely. I apologized again for the way things ended, but I haven't spoken to her since then."

"I'm sorry you had to go through that, Chase. That had to be stressful and heartbreaking…for both of you," Chivonne said.

"Yeah, it was, but after we broke up, I realized that I had been more stressed out thinking about marrying her than I was after we broke up. I definitely got free, for sure!"

"Is it wrong for me to say that I'm glad that it didn't work out?" Chivonne asked, timidly.

"Not at all, Chivonne. Not at all," he answered, smiling and looking down at the ground. Chivonne got up from the ground and they continued walking.

Chivonne and Chase spent a few hours walking up and down the park trail, sharing childhood memories and their visions for the future. Chivonne shared with Chase what it took to make the move from Philly to Los Angeles, all alone, and how terrified she was to be leaving everything and everyone she knew back home. Chase talked about how he almost moved across the country after his engagement ended and how God told him to stay in LA. At the time, he didn't understand why it was so important for him to stay in LA, as opposed to starting over in another city, but he decided to trust God and believe that God knew what was best for him. The time they spent at that very moment, sharing their lives and getting to know each other better, was something they both deeply desired to experience with each other. They both hoped, and somehow knew, that this would be the beginning of something beautiful.

Chase invited Chivonne to his mother's birthday dinner later that night. He had never casually brought women around his family, so he knew exactly what to expect once they arrived—that his family would be surprised that he would actually bring someone to his mother's house. As expected, they were shocked to discover that Chivonne and Chase had met only the night before. After his last relationship ended, Chase made every effort to avoid women, as difficult as it was, let alone actually bring one home to his family.

Surprised by his unusual behavior, his mother pulled him aside during dinner. "Why on earth would someone in his right mind bring someone that he just met, to meet his family so soon," she asked him, "and why *this* girl?"

Without giving away too many details, because he didn't have many details, he explained to his mother that there was something special about Chivonne and that she was unlike any other woman he had ever met before. He let her know that she needed to trust him and trust that he would only do what God directed him to do. He reassured her that he was not moving too fast and that he was, indeed, in his right mind. In fact, aside from giving his life to Christ ten years before, Chase had never been so sure about anything in his life. He did not want to jump to conclusions, so he made sure not to move too fast with Chivonne. She had become very special to him, very quickly.

During dinner that night, Chivonne stayed close by Chase and he made sure to let her know that she was welcomed, although she felt like she was getting side-eyes from everyone in the room. Jennifer was the only person at the party that she knew besides Chase, and even she seemed to be busy reuniting with family members she hadn't seen in months. Taking in as much as she could about Chase's family, Chivonne scanned the room, eavesdropping on several conversations. This was a new experience and somewhat terrifying for her, being around the family of a new guy. She was, however, able to muster up a little bit of calm in the midst of the storm, knowing that this new guy was not just *any* guy.

5

"Are you serious?"

"Yes, I'm serious. Why?" Chivonne asked.

"I go to Faith Church, too! I've never seen you there! Why am I just now finding this out?" Chase answered, almost yelling.

"Are *you* serious? I did not know that you attend Faith Church and I have never seen you there either!"

"Have you always been there or did you just recently join?" he asked.

"I've been there for a couple months, I think. Now that I think about it, your cousin did mention that we attend the same church when she introduced us that night, remember?"

"No, I do not remember that at all. Where was *I* that night? Better yet, where was my mind that night? I must have been so love struck that I missed everything but your name."

"Love struck?" Chivonne asked, reluctantly.

"Uh, yeah. You know, love struck. Awestruck. Struck by love. Mesmerized. All that good stuff! I had a real connection to you that night. It wasn't forced or fake. It felt real. It felt *good*. It felt like something that I haven't felt in a while—or maybe even at all. It was pretty much love at first sight for me. I was in." Chase found himself gazing into her eyes as he spoke.

"So why have I not seen you at church before?" Chivonne asked, quickly changing the subject. "Aren't you the youth minister?"

"Yes, I am a youth minister," Chases uttered, still gazing at her. "I teach Sunday school on some Sundays and Bible study at midweek service for the youth, so you'll rarely see me if you're over the age of thirteen! And, are you just going to act like I did not just tell you that I'm in love with you?"

"No, Chase. I'm not acting like anything! Anyway, how is it that we have been attending the same church this entire time and have never crossed paths?"

"Well, it *is* a fairly large church. And I would not necessarily say that we have never crossed each other's paths. I had seen you before the night we met, just not at church."

"Really? When?! Where?!" Chivonne shouted. "When did you see me? Where was I? How long ago? What was I wearing? Was my hair done? What did I look like?" Chivonne was eager for answers. She felt like she was *dying* to know.

"Whoa! Relax! So many questions, and I honestly cannot answer most of them. Well, I saw you in my dreams, first and foremost!" he said, jokingly, with the biggest grin his cheekbones would allow. "But, in reality, I saw you at the market downtown about a month before we met and again at the market on the day we met. I was doing some shopping and I saw you sitting on the bench outside of the Casual Male clothing store. I figured since you were waiting outside the men's clothing store that you were probably waiting for *your* man to come out."

"Why didn't you say anything to me?" she asked.

"When I saw you those times or after we met?" he inquired.

"Either," Chivonne replied softly, finally able to look Chase in his eyes.

"Well, that's not really my style, you know, trying to holler at a woman on the street," Chase responded. "And like I said, I assumed you were with your husband slash fiancé slash boyfriend. So, that was the end of it for me."

"So what made you change your mind the night we met?" Chivonne asked.

"I guess I was just shocked that I actually saw you again and I figured that since I saw you again that I should probably see what all the hype was about!" Chase expressed in excitement. "And, I was ditched for a blind date the night before! It kind of had me bummed out, so I may have been trying to redeem myself!"

"Oh." Chivonne did not have much of a response considering she *was* actually shopping with a man that afternoon. She was, however, relieved that Chase did not see her with Trey, or that he decided not to mention it. "You had a blind date the night before we met?" she asked.

"Well, not exactly. A few of my co-workers had gotten together at a lounge downtown and one of them wanted me to meet her friend. But, her friend never showed up."

"Really?" Chivonne asked.

"Yeah, I thought that was kind of rude of her not to show up after she said she would," Chase answered.

"Hmmm. Yeah, I guess you're right. I wonder why she didn't show up."

"Your guess is better than mine."

6

A week later

"Pastor Young! Do you have a minute? There's someone I'd like you to meet," Chase shouted, as he and Chivonne walked towards Pastor Young's office.

"Oh, who is this beautiful young lady you have here on your arm?" Pastor Young asked, motioning for Chase to bring her in.

"This is Chivonne," Chase said, smiling and holding her arm close to his side, with his eyes glued to her.

"Good to finally meet you, Pastor Young! I've been coming here for a couple months, but have never had the opportunity to meet you. I really love this church!"

"Thank you, sweetheart! And it's a pleasure to meet you as well. I'm glad you've enjoyed so far."

"Absolutely! I'm glad I found a church home here in LA, since I just moved here a few months ago."

"Oh, that's awesome, Chivonne! Well, listen. I've got to get going shortly, but Chase, why don't you bring Chivonne by the house next Sunday for dinner after service. Sound good?"

"Yes sir! Sounds good. I'll talk to you soon," Chase answered. Chivonne and Chase left Pastor Young's office.

Later that night, Pastor Young called Chase. "Chase, how's everything?"

"Everything is great. What's going on?"

"After you left my office today, God showed me a few things that I want to share with you."

"Okay. I'm all ears!"

"You already know that Chivonne is the woman that you will marry. But, I want to let you know that the process of courting and your engagement will not be very long. As long as you both keep God at the core of your relationship and continue to seek his guidance, he will direct your steps and move you quickly into your marriage. He has prepared you both for this process, Chase. Don't be afraid to ask him for direction for even what to wear, where to go, and what to say to her. Be intentional in your conversation and sincere with your intentions. Speak from your heart, but be led by the Holy Spirit. He knows exactly what you need and exactly what you need to do in order to be successful in your marriage."

"Okay." Chase was somewhat surprised at how direct Pastor Young was.

"Now, listen Chase. Even your close friends and family will question this relationship because they will not understand how everything could happen so quickly, but trust God, Chase. Just trust God."

"I understand completely, Pastor Young. God has been showing me exactly what you just said. He's been teaching me so many things lately and showing me how to stay focused on what he said, and not on what everyone else has to say about my life and my decisions. I'm so ready! And, I thank you for the confirmation! But, I do have just one question. How did you know that God already told me that Chivonne will be my wife?"

"Son, I've been walking with the Lord longer than you have been alive. He lets me in on secrets I wouldn't share with anyone unless he instructs me to do so. And, she's beautiful and meets every bullet point that you have on your list. Your ex didn't. when you brought Chivonne into my office to meet me, I noticed you looking at her in a way that I have never seen you look at any woman, even when you were just a teenager. You have never held any young lady with such high esteem. And Chase, game recognizes game, son! That's how I know!"

"Ha! Yes sir. And you are the original player and creator of the game, so you definitely should be able to recognize it!"

"And don't you forget it. Enjoy the rest of your evening, Chase."

"You too."

7

June 1

As Chivonne and Chase made their way into the room where Chase would be teaching Bible study that night, the room filled quickly with energetic "tweens" and teenagers. Chivonne took a seat near the back of the room, as Chase headed to the front.

"Okay guys. Let's take our seats and get ready to start tonight's Bible study. We've got a lot of ground to cover and I don't want to hold you guys too long. I know you've got to get home and watch your favorite television shows, not to mention it is a school night!" Chase, too, wanted to begin and finish just as quickly as they did, but not for the same reasons. He had invited Chivonne to visit the teen ministry that night and he wanted to make sure that he would have as much time as he could to spend with Chivonne after service, before it got too late.

"Alright. Tonight we are going to talk about trust and learning how to trust in God and his plan for your life. Let's look at—"

"—Oh, I know! I know! Proverbs three, verse five!" one of the kids yelled.

"You're absolutely right! Someone has been reading ahead, I see," Chase said, while bringing up the scripture on his tablet. "Proverbs chapter three and page twenty-seven in your workbooks. Let's begin at verse five and we'll keep reading until I say to stop. And since I see a lot of new faces tonight, let me first explain how this works. First, we'll all take five minutes of quiet time to read to ourselves, to make sure we understand the scripture and understand what God is telling us through the scripture. In your workbooks, I want you to jot down anything that stands out to you or anything you hear God tell you. This is God's word to us. It's one of the ways he speaks to us, so it is important for us to understand what He's saying. And if you didn't get a workbook when you came in, it's okay. You can take notes on your phone because I know you guys have them! Okay, let's read."

"Trust God from the bottom of your heart. Don't try to figure out everything on your own. Listen for God's voice in everything you do, everywhere you go; he's the one who will keep you on track. Don't assume that you know it all. Run to God! Run from evil! Your body will glow with health; your very bones will vibrate with life! Honor God with everything you own; give him the first and best." (Proverbs 3:5-9 MSG)

"Okay, stop!" Chase interjected. "Alright, so now let's take five to read the same verses we just read, quietly to ourselves. As you're reading, really try to capture every word and read each sentence until you understand it completely. If you have to read it several times over, do that. This is for you. No one else has to know how many times you're reading it or what you're getting out of it. What you're reading and writing is for you and only you. Let's take five."

Each time that Chase taught teen Bible study, he really wanted them to understand the meaning and significance of each word they were reading. His "Take 5" method was something he began doing with the teens a few months before, and it helped him to gauge their level of understanding before he even opened his mouth to speak. He wanted to know that they were not just reading and memorizing the scripture, but that they were really thinking about what they were reading. This method of teaching really helped him to become comfortable with them and it helped them because he was able to teach at the level they were on each night. He never wanted to say anything beyond what God gave him to share and what they would be able to receive.

"Alright. Let's get started. Would anyone like to share what they got from this scripture?" Chase asked.

"I'll share," one of the kids said quietly, with his hand raised high.

"Okay. Let's hear it! What does this scripture mean to you and what stood out to you, if anything?"

"What this scripture means to me is that God knows what I need. I have to trust Him completely, and the rest is laid out for me. Pretty much, I won't have to worry about what I need to do if I trust God to lead me."

"Wow! Thank you for sharing that." Chase was amazed at such a wise yet simple understanding. "Okay, then. So, let's talk about that. God has promised us an abundant, prosperous, and blessed life. He knows what we need to do in order to receive and live that life. He knows what we need...and what we don't need, for that matter. And like this wise young man has so beautifully stated, everything is all laid out for us when we trust God. If we continue to read a little further down, we see that when we trust God we will receive more than our little minds can dream of and we will live in the overflow of His love and blessings. And in all of that, Solomon, who wrote the book of Proverbs, warns us to not resent God's discipline and correction because He loves us and only wants His best for us. When we do something wrong, it is because God loves us so much that He corrects us and keeps us on the right track."

As Chivonne sat in the back of the room, listening intently, she realized that she was not only learning, but she, too, was receiving exactly what she needed that night. She had heard and read that same scripture many times before, but with everything that had been happening in her life recently, she had been quietly struggling with fully trusting God to lead her and show her how to live the blessed life that he promised. She knew that she was exactly where she wanted to be and that things were somehow working out, but she needed to know for sure that she was where God wanted her to be and that is was God who was working things out on her behalf.

Chivonne was amazed that night at how God was teaching her the same thing that he was teaching a room full of teenagers. She hadn't shared any of her struggles with Chase, yet he was so tuned in to what God wanted to say to those kids and to her.

It was important for Chivonne to be able to see the type of man that Chase was, apart from her and their new relationship. She never wanted to be so into Chase that she would not be able to see the reality of who he was and if he really had a heart for ministry. He spoke so many great things, but she wanted to see for herself just how great he really was. She needed to see it and experience it. She needed to know that this man would be fit to lead their family one day, should that time ever come.

After Bible study, Chase drove Chivonne home after they grabbed a quick bite to eat at a nearby fast food restaurant.

"Have you told your sister about us yet?" Chase asked, just before Chivonne opened his car door to get out.

"Not yet...I mean...I've been meaning to tell her, and my mom, but I'm honestly just afraid," she answered.

"What are you afraid of?" Chase questioned.

"Everything has been moving so fast between us and I guess I'm just afraid that they won't support me, or us. They're the closest to me and...well...if they don't support me, then I'm not sure what to do. I guess I'm just waiting for the perfect time."

"Chivonne, there will never be a perfect time to do anything. When you're prepared and obedient to God, that's the perfect time!" He paused, looking over at her. "Are you unsure about you and me?"

"Not really, no," she answered, looking back over at Chase. "At least I don't think I'm unsure. I love what we have. And, I'm sure of it. I'm sure of you! I just don't know how to say it to them."

"Just say it."

Chivonne and Chase spent almost every day together, but Chivonne did not consume herself with the "what if?", "when?", or "how?" concerning their rapidly growing relationship. Although they were still in the "newness" phase of their relationship, they were both comfortable with how much time they were spending together. It was also very important to them both to move slowly, get to know each other as friends, and allow the relationship to develop naturally.

With all of the excitement, it was awfully difficult for Chivonne to keep such a deep secret from her sister, whom she told almost everything. They spoke on the phone daily and always talked about everything going on with each other. Withholding details about the amazing guy she was spending almost every day with was no easy task. Knowing that the longer she waited, the more upset her sister would be with her for not telling her, she decided to call her sister that night to tell her about Chase.

"Hey Blair! Sorry for calling you so late. I just got home," she began.

"Oh, it's fine. I'm up. What's going on?" her sister asked.

"I have a confession to make," Chivonne, said, very slowly, still hesitating on whether or not to bring up the subject of her new love life.

"You're pregnant!" her sister screamed.

"No, Blair! I am not pregnant. Considering I am not married yet, that would be impossible," Chivonne responded, in disdain.

"Not impossible, but definitely something we would have to talk about. Then what's your confession?"

"I met someone."

"*That's* your confession?" Blair said, sounding annoyed.

"A guy. A *man*. About a month and a half ago."

"And you are just now telling me, your beloved big sister? Your *only* sister? You've been seeing this guy for a whole month and a half and I am just now finding out about him? What has our relationship come to, Chivonne?"

"Relax Blair. Jeez! I didn't tell you until today because I didn't want to talk about it and end up disappointed again. You know how much I hate the dating scene. Honestly, I've been in prayer about this for the past two weeks because I refuse to be out of God's will or end up wishing I were single again."

With every colorful detail and dramatic scene included, painting the picture of her and Chase was easy. Chivonne enjoyed telling her sister about all of the fun she had been having over the past few weeks and how much she and Chase had learned about each other in such a short time.

"We've been spending a lot of time together, pretty much since we met, and I'm really starting to like him," she began. "The night we met, we talked on the phone until the next morning. I met his family the very next day, and—"

"—Wait! What? You met his family the day after you met him? Blair asked, demanding to know. "It sounds like you guys really hit it off! So, where did you meet him? How did this all happen? I feel like I don't even know you!" her sister shouted.

"I know, right? It's all kind of surreal, but, trust me, I have not been doing it alone. I have been praying about everything and God has been showing me that I'm moving in the right direction. He is such an amazing person, outside of being really, really cute! He loves his family and he mentors kids at church. He actually attends the same church that I do, but we met at a concert I went to about a month and a half ago. I had never seen him at church before the day we met."

"Really?" Blair asked. "Well, maybe you had seen him before in passing, but never noticed him."

"Blair, he is like 6'4 and really, really cute! I find it hard to believe that I would not have noticed him at church if I had actually seen him," Chivonne declared.

"Well, sometimes God will not allow us to have something until He knows that we are ready to receive it and sometimes He will not allow us to see something that is for us until He knows that we are ready for it."

"You could be right. But, it's still sort of crazy to know that he was right there the entire time, and it took me being somewhere else to actually meet him. I have waited so long for this time to come and it's all finally happening, you know?"

"Yeah, I definitely understand."

"And there's one other thing. I think he was the guy I was supposed to meet on that blind date that I ditched."

"No way! Are you serious? How do you know? Did you ask him?" Blair inquired.

"No, I haven't asked him yet. He mentioned something about his co-workers meeting the night before we met and how he was supposed to meet his co-worker's friend, but the friend never showed up. I'm pretty sure I'm the friend who didn't show."

"People meet for blind dates all the time, Chivonne. How do you know it was the one that *you* ditched? And wouldn't he know by now, since he knows your name?" Blair questioned.

"He said his co-worker never told him the girl's name. And he didn't mention the co-worker's name, so I'm not sure it was my neighbor, Kye, that he was referring to."

Chivonne and her sister continued to talk about everything that happened, from meeting Chase's family to enjoying dinner dates with friends, which was especially exciting for Chivonne because she was able to see Chase for who he was, outside of her.

Chivonne told Blair what happened at Bible study that night and about meeting the pastor earlier that week.

"Even though Chase has a great relationship with his own father, he looks up to our pastor. Pastor Young is a close friend of Chase's dad, so he knows him pretty well. He said that when it comes to relationships and dating advice, he knows where to go, because Pastor Young was partly responsible for helping save Chase's mom and dad's marriage," Chivonne explained.

"That is interesting," Blair chimed in.

"Yeah, and he knows that he has his best interest in mind. Chase says that if Pastor Young approves of our relationship, then he and I are on the right track! Oh, one more thing! Chase was engaged before."

"Are you serious? What happened with that?" Blair asked.

"Yeah, I'm serious. He did tell me some of what caused him to break off his engagement and how he now realizes that it was the best decision he could have made, so I'm not stressing over it. Things happen, you know? I can't hold that against him."

"Yeah, everybody has a past. Good or bad."

"One thing he did mention is that he had wondered why God would allow him to go through a five-year long relationship to only have it end just three months before the day of the wedding. He had gone through a time where he blamed God for not telling him not to date her from the beginning, but he admits that he pursued the relationship without ever asking God about her in the first place."

"Yeah, that makes sense."

"Pastor Young knows all about what Chase went through with his ex and that she was not the woman that God had for him. However, he knew Chase was not looking for a relationship so soon, so it surprised him when he brought me into his office."

"I can imagine that he *would* be surprised!" Blair exclaimed. "He most likely cares for him far too much to watch him make a decision that could have potentially caused him to be miserable for the rest of his life," she added.

"Yeah, it wasn't until Chase asked him to perform the wedding ceremony that Pastor Young told him how he felt."

8

June 18

"Hey, can you see me?" Chivonne asked.

"No! I can't. I don't know how to use this thing," her mom replied.

"Mom, tap the screen in the bottom corner to flip your camera around." Chivonne waited.

"Oh, okay. There you are. Hey Chivonne! How are you, sweetie?"

"Hey ma! I'm good! Is Blair with you?"

"Hey Chivonne! I'm here!" Blair shouted from the background.

"Okay, great! Blair, come to the phone really quickly so I can see you. I have something I want you both to see!" Chivonne began, pushing her tablet away from her face to show a wider view of where she was. "This is Chase," she continued, aiming the front-facing camera at him.

"Hi Ms. Wilson. Good to meet you!" he said.

"Why hello there Chase! It's a pleasure to finally meet the man who has been occupying all of my daughter's time!" her mom replied.

"Oh, Chivonne, he *is* cute!" Blair chimed in, as she walked up to the phone to get a better look at him. Chase smiled.

"Thank you!" he said.

"Yes, a very handsome young man you are, Chase," her mom added. "You two be careful out here, looking all good together! Things might get tricky and you two don't want to slip and fall, if you know what I mean!"

"Karen Wilson! Please stop before you scare him away! We will be fine! We know our boundaries," Chivonne replied, already feeling embarrassed. Blair snickered from the background.

"You see that, Chase?! She thinks she can call me by my full name to shut me up! I'm just trying to help you young folks not to shack up! Holiness is still right!"

"Ha! Okay, ma. That's enough! Please hand Blair the phone…"

9

A month later

"Blair, I said yes!"

"Yes to what?" she asked.

"To Chase! He proposed at breakfast this morning! I cannot believe this is finally happening!"

"Congratulations!" Blair said, excitedly. "I have to admit I knew about the proposal. Chase called me a couple weeks ago to talk to mom and me and ask for our blessing...and your ring size! We were so shocked, since the only time we ever spoke to him was that time you put us all on video calling."

"Wow! I wondered how he knew exactly what size ring to buy. And he *was* acting a bit strange when he asked to use my phone a couple weeks ago. This is crazy!"

"I know!"

"I guess the answer is obvious, but what was mom's reaction? How did she respond to him asking you two?"

"She actually surprised me! I thought she would have asked him why he was in such a hurry to marry you, but I think he charmed her enough that night that she fell in love with him, too!" Blair answered.

"You know, that doesn't surprise me because she has been trying to marry me off since I graduated from college. She is probably ecstatic about the whole thing! The quicker I'm married, the less she has to worry about when or *if* I'd actually get married!"

"Yeah, that's mom for you! I wish I could have been there for the proposal. It's all happening so fast, but I know that he is the man that God has for you."

"He better be that man, considering how long I've waited. But, I cannot even believe that it has only been three months. It's crazy!"

As Chivonne and her sister continued to chat about the engagement, dabbling in a bit of wedding planning details, Chivonne pulled up into the driveway of Chase's parents' house to meet him and his family for dinner.

"You know I've only ever wanted a small wedding. I'm thinking no more than ten people from both sides, combined!" she exclaimed.

"Girl, that is unrealistic! *You* may only have five people that you want to invite to your wedding, but what about *his* family? And *his* friends? And whoever else may be part of his life? He may have a long list of people he wants to be there. You have to consider that, too."

"I know," Chivonne replied, "but, I still want to keep it as small as possible. I'm not into all the hoopla, you know? I just want to have a very private and intimate wedding. Nothing too big. I want to keep my private affairs private."

"I hear you on that one!"

"Anyway, Chase just pulled up so I'll have to talk to you later. We're meeting his family for dinner. I'll give you a ring as soon as I get home."

"OK. Love you lil' sis."

"I love you, too, Blair. Talk to you later."

As Chivonne ended the call with her sister, Chase was standing by her driver's side window.

"Hey beautiful," he said through the window.

"Hey!" she answered, as Chase pulled her car door open.

She loved that Chase called her "beautiful" as if it were her name. It was one of the things that he did that made her feel like he adored her.

"Before we go in, I have to warn you about something. I just found out that my aunts are in town, and they will be at dinner tonight...and they are wild...and loud...very loud," Chase began, as Chivonne stepped out of the car. He shut the car door behind her.

"Okay, thank you for the warning, after I agree to become part of your very wild and loud family!"

"I honestly did not know that they were going to be here this weekend, but my dad just called me and told me that they stopped by unannounced. This should be very interesting, to say the least."

"Well, I'm not so sure I want to go in now! What if they don't like me?" she asked.

"Chivonne, don't be silly. I'm positive that they will love you just as much as I do," Chase said, confidently, grabbing her left hand and pulling her towards him as they walked toward the house. They were greeted at the door by Chase's dad, who introduced Chivonne to his sisters-in-law, Chase's *wild and loud* aunts. Chase's eldest aunt, Patricia, was Chase's favorite, and the loudest of them all. Aunt Patricia never really liked his ex, Tamara, and she made sure he knew it on several occasions...sometimes in front of her. She loved her nephew and always wanted the best for him. She somehow always knew that Tamara was not what was best for him.

It was important to Chase that his family accepted Chivonne because she had become very special to him. He wanted everyone to get along and for everyone to love her. Mostly everyone seemed to, except his Aunt Patricia.

"She's cute, I guess. She looks bougie…too prim and proper, like she's better than everyone else. I don't like her!" Aunt Pat began, standing next to Chase with her arms crossed, while he made a plate of food.

"Aunt Pat, you haven't even tried talking to her yet. How can you not like her? Give her a chance, will you?" Chase pleaded.

"This is my sister's house! I don't have to speak to her. *She* should be speaking to *me*!"

"You're right. This is your sister's house, not *your* house. And Chivonne is a guest…my guest. Please do not be rude to her. I love this girl and I do not need you guys scaring her away!

"*Love?* You just met her like ten minutes ago!" Aunt Pat said, sarcastically. "How could you possibly love her already? You probably don't even know her last name yet?"

"As a matter of fact, I do. And I know her middle name, too. *Chivonne Lourdes Wilson*! And for your information, we met three months ago."

"*Lourdes?* What does that even mean? I bet she doesn't even know what it means. Go and ask her!" Aunt Patricia shouted, uncrossing her arms to point toward Chivonne.

"Aunt Patricia! Don't be so loud! And who cares whether or not I know her middle name or even her last name, for that matter. All that matters is that very soon she'll have *my* last name," Chase scorned his aunt, as he picked up his plate and headed towards the dining room. "What brought you to town all unannounced anyway?" Aunt Patricia followed. They both took a seat at the dining room table, a couple seats down and across from Chivonne, who seemed to be getting an earful from one of Chase's other aunts.

"Well, Chase, your poor mother called me a couple of weeks ago, going on and on about this bougie girl that her eldest son is now quote, *going with*, unquote. And, well, we wanted to see for ourselves just how bougie she really is!"

"Really, Aunt Pat? Going with? You must be stuck in the nineties with your daughter, who told me to quote, *get those digits*, unquote! Who still says that? Chase laughed. "And please stop calling her bougie."

"I still say it, Chase. And your mother, apparently! We cannot keep up with you young folks with your social media and your trap music. I can't keep up!" Aunt Pat snapped.

"Ha! Even I cannot keep up with trap music, Aunt Pat, so I am with you on that!"

Although hiding it well, Chase was becoming uneasy with keeping the engagement a secret though dinner because he wanted to share the great news with everyone. As he decided to make his announcement before it got too late, he got up and walked around the table towards Chivonne.

"Can I have everyone's attention please? I have an announcement to make. *We* have an announcement to make," pulling Chivonne out of her seat.

"She's pregnant?" one of Chase's other aunts shouted.

"No! She isn't pregnant, but that may change sooner than later. But, what did happen is that this morning I made the best decision of my life, next to accepting Christ, of course, and I asked this beautiful young lady to spend the rest of her life with me."

"You're engaged?"

"Yes, mom, *we* are engaged!" Chase answered.

"I mean, you did tell your father and me that you were going to ask her to marry you, but I certainly did not believe that you would go through with it so soon, Chase."

The room became uncomfortably quiet, as each family member slowly looked around at each other, unsure of what Chase could possibly say next. After what seemed like a lifetime of silence, Chase's mom continued before he could respond.

"That was quick. Why so soon? You have only been dating for what, three months? Don't you think that's a little too fast to decide that you want to marry someone, Chase?"

"Well, no, not really…especially if you've been spending as much time together as we have. And we have been spending a lot of time together, mom. When God sends someone into your life and shows you that this person is right for you and that it's the right time, then you move when He says move. Not a minute later!"

With the exception of Jennifer, who had introduced Chivonne and Chase, everyone seemed a little more surprised and less happy about the announcement. The excitement died rather quickly for Chivonne and Chase, as they were disappointed with his family's reaction.

What should have been a moment filled with happiness and well-wishes, the minutes following the announcement were filled with various side conversations between family members—the engagement as the obvious topic of choice, as well as the elephant in the room. Chivonne and Chase decided to make an early departure and began to say their quick goodbyes—but not before and unexpected guest arrived.

"Look who's here! This should be interesting!" Aunt Pat mumbled.

"Hi Chase, how are you?"

As surprised as everyone else, he stood with a blank stare, but no answer.

"Who is that, Chase?" Chivonne whispered.

"That's Tamara, my ex," he answered.

"Why is she here?" she asked.

"Your guess is better than mine," he answered, looking away.

"Tamara, so nice to see you, sweetie," Chase's mom shouted, with excitement, pulling her aside. "I'm glad you could make it! I had no idea there would be so many *other* people here, but I'm glad you came!"

"It's nice to see you, too, Mrs. Hendricks, but what's going on here?" Tamara asked, peeping back at Chase and Chivonne. "Who is that standing next to Chase?" she continued.

"Just his little girlfriend. I didn't know that she would be here. Well, I did, but I didn't think they were as serious as they are. And she's his *fiancé* now, or so they just announced."

"His *fiancé*?! With all due respect, Mrs. Hendricks, then why did you invite me here?!" Tamara asked.

"I just thought you'd like to see Chase again. And I thought that if he saw you then he would remember all the fun times you two had together and he'd forget all about *what's her name.*"

"O...kay. Well, I guess that one went out the window. This is so embarrassing...and awkward!" Tamara replied, nervously running her fingers through her hair, looking down at the floor.

"Listen, sweetie. Maybe you should just talk to him. Will you at least do that?"

"I really don't think that's appropriate. He's here with his new fiancé and I'm his *ex*-fiancé . I'm embarrassed enough already! I should just leave."

"No, no! Don't leave just yet. Just go and mingle a little." Mrs. Hendricks insisted that Tamara chat with Chase, motioning for her to walk towards him. "It has been so long since you've been around and I know you must be tired from traveling. Just stay a little while…and talk to Chase a little bit."

"Mrs. Hendricks, you know I have the greatest respect for you. But, the truth of the matter is that no matter how much you and I want Chase back into my life, he has clearly moved on. And besides, I treated him so badly when he called the wedding off. I'm pretty sure he doesn't want to hear what I have to say anyway. I'm gonna go." Not waiting for Mrs. Hendricks to respond, Tamara headed for the front door and waved goodbye to Chase's dad on the way out.

10

Later that night

"Chase, did anyone even say congratulations?"

"Not that I can remember. It's all a blur to me right now!

"I certainly did not expect tonight to go the way it did. I was hoping that everyone would be excited for you and be a little more welcoming of me. I was especially surprised by the special guest," Chivonne added.

"I know, right? My mom is something else! I cannot believe she invited my ex!" Chase replied.

"Why would she do that? What did she expect to happen? Your mom is *really* not happy about me being in your life, is she?"

"I don't know what she expects, but she'll have to get over it. You're gonna be around and she'll just have to deal! Besides, she's more upset that Tamara is out of my life than she is about you being in it. That's her problem."

"But, what is it about Tamara that she loves so much, and that she doesn't see in me?" she asked.

"Chivonne, this is not about you. My mom's silly behavior tonight has nothing to do with you. She couldn't possibly see what I see in you and the reason why I love you because she hasn't made any effort to. Please don't think this is about anything being wrong with you!" Chase assured her.

"And your Aunt Pat hates me. What is *that* about?"

Chase was silent.

"Hello?"

"Yeah, I'm here."

"Why does your aunt hate me?"

"She doesn't hate you, Chivonne. She just doesn't know you yet and she has a hard time liking people that she doesn't know that well. That's all."

"I mean, did something happen with Tamara that made her act that way towards *me*?"

"No. Not really."

Chivonne waited for Chase to continue, but he didn't.

"Chase, you're unusually quiet tonight. What's going on? Talk to me Ch—"

"—I'm just really drained after tonight and I'm a little upset about everything that happened…or didn't happen. I don't want to take my frustrations out on you so I'll just call it a night and we'll talk about it tomorrow," Chase said, abruptly. "I—I'll just talk to you tomorrow."

Chivonne desperately wanted to respond, hoping that Chase would open up to her in that moment. Although she did not want the conversation to end that way, she had remembered from past experiences that she needed to give him the time and space to think things out on his own. However, she wanted Chase to know that he could be completely vulnerable with her about what he was feeling. She was concerned about how the night's events made him feel, but she knew that whatever Chase was going through, he had to get through on his own. She made it clear to him that she was ready and willing to listen whenever he was ready to talk.

"Call me tomorrow or come by. I'll be home all day," she said.

"Okay, I'll see you tomorrow. Goodnight."

"Goodnight, Chase."

As Chivonne got ready for bed, so many thoughts raced through her mind about what happened that night. Although she was excited about the engagement, she was confused about how Chase's family reacted, his mom especially. She had hoped that Chase's family would accept her just like her family loved and embraced him. She made sure to send up and extra special prayer for him that night.

"Dear Lord...I have no idea what I'm doing. I'm thankful that you have brought Chase into my life, but I have no idea what I am doing with him. If this relationship is your will, then why are there so many people against it? Why can't everyone else see how you brought us together, and just be happy for us? Okay, Lord. I know. Not everyone is focused on you and not everyone wants to be in your will. I get that. But, when something is right, everyone else should see that it's right, right? God, I believe that you brought us together and we know that you have told us both that we are for each other, but God, please help my unbelief when things get rough and the haters start hating! I'll keep holding on to the word you gave me and I pray that Chase will hold on to what you spoke to him. I love you and thank you for your grace, as you have and continue to set things in place for us. I will trust in you to lead me in the way that I should go. I have no choice but to trust you because I don't know what else to do. Thank you, Lord, for your love and your grace and your favor and your blessings and everything you have done for me and Chase. Have your way in our lives. In Jesus' name, Amen."

11

Four days later

Chivonne woke up early to begin searching online for a wedding dress. She always had an idea of what she would want to wear, but because she thought she might not ever meet a decent man, she had never put any real effort into looking for a wedding gown. This was all a new experience. The wedding was round the corner and would be here before she knew it, so she wanted to get an early start. From choosing a dress to finding the perfect reception hall, all of the wedding details were becoming a bit overwhelming, with the big day just two months away.

While Chivonne wrapped up plans for her wedding dress, faster than the speed of sound, Chase stopped by his parents' house to talk to them about the engagement. After pulling up to the house, he sat in the car for a few minutes, unsure of what to say or how to even begin. After a short while, he decided to go inside.

"Hey son, come on in."

"Hey mom. How are you?"

"I'm doing alright. You look great, son! Are you working out again?" his mom asked.

"Yeah, Chivonne has me on this new fitness plan that has me looking all thin and malnourished lately, but I feel great!"

"I guess whatever that girl has you doing is working, huh?"

Somewhat offended by how his mother addressed his new fiancé, Chase wanted to chide her, but he wanted more to avoid the argument.

"What are all these boxes for?" he asked, instead.

"Your dad and I have been doing some work around the house, trying to clear out some things. You know how it gets in the house during the summer. We're getting up there in age, so we want to make sure we can breathe and move around this house like you young folks can."

"Ha! Yeah, I know. That's good. Don't throw out my old basketball trophies, though. Those will be worth something, twenty years from now. I'm just saying! I can still hoop!"

"Don't worry, son. Your dad made sure that I kept those. He wouldn't dare let me throw out your trophies. He's very proud of you and all of your accomplishments. He's proud of all of you."

"I know, mom. I know."

Avoiding the conversation that he knew he needed to have with his mother, Chase knew that putting it off longer would only make it more difficult to have once they finally did. He desperately wanted his mom to mention it first.

Chase and his mother chatted for a few minutes until he had to leave and meet Chivonne at the bakery to taste wedding cake samples.

"Well…I've got to get going. I'm supposed to meet Chivonne in a few minutes and I don't want to be late. I love you mom," he mumbled, walking towards the front door.

"I love you, too, son. Don't be a stranger around here. I'll tell your dad that you stopped by."

"Okay, mom. I'll give dad a call a bit later."

It pained Chase to not talk about the issues at hand, but it did not come as easily as he had wished. Eventually, he would have to be upfront and honest with his mom about the fact that she needed to get over his past relationship. He knew that the only reason she was not happy for him and Chivonne was because she still wanted him to marry his ex. His mom loved Tamara sand was distraught when the relationship ended. She was very much involved with planning the wedding because she never had a wedding of her own. Chase having broken off the engagement, really took a toll on his relationship with his mother, so he could certainly understand how she would be upset about how quickly he became engaged to someone else. He knew that he had to be patient with his mom and make every effort to make this process easier for her.

Chase arrived at the bakery where he and Chivonne were to meet with the wedding cake coordinator. Chase was not too fond of wedding planning, probably because he had such a difficult time planning the wedding that never happened. An oversized church full of people was what his ex and mom wanted. Something small and intimate, no more than ten guests and the woman he loved, was his idea of the perfect wedding.

"Hey beautiful!"

Chivonne turned around to find Chase standing there. "Hey handsome! Sorry to keep you waiting. I ran into some traffic on the 405. You know how that LA traffic can be."

"It's cool. I was just sitting in my car going over some notes for church tonight when I saw you walk inside."

"Oh, okay. Have I told you how much I love seeing you teach? Your teaching style is so seamless and it's really easy for me to stay engaged in what you're saying. And those teens love you! I see why Pastor Young asked you to teach Sunday school and Bible study, because you're pretty much amazing, Chase! And I'm not just saying that because I sort of like you!"

"Sort of? Oh, now you just *sort of* like me, huh?" Chase laughed.

"Well, you know. I just *sorta kinda* have a crush on my fiancé because he's *sorta kinda* cute. Just a little bit!" Chivonne whispered, sliding her right arm into his left arm, resting her chin on his shoulder. Chase beamed as he stared into her eyes, not saying a word. "Do you have any idea how special you are, Chase? She asked. "I love how much you love your family and the respect you have for your parents and how much you love the kids you teach every week. I love how much you love the word of God! I've never met someone, especially a man, who has such a good heart and cares for everyone around him. And I appreciate you for being intentional in this relationship. You have been very straight-forward with where you want us to go and about us growing together. I mean, I did ask God for a man like you, but I guess I never believed that it could happen. You're truly one of a kind! Did I mention that you are *fiiine*, too?" Chivonne asked, still holding onto his arm.

"Don't make me blush out here in these streets! You know I have an image to uphold!" Chase replied.

"What image? Boy, come and sit down so we can taste some cake," she snickered, letting go of his arm and walking towards the counter. Chase followed behind her. "I am so hungry right now, I could eat a whole cake by myself!" she added.

"You had better not be eating any cake other than *this* cake, with this diet you have *me* on. I'm hungrier than a hostage!"

Chivonne and Chase sat down at the tasting bar and were immediately overwhelmed with all of the cake displays. From chocolate with vanilla icing and strawberry with coconut icing to lace and fondant designs, they had no idea what to choose or where to even begin.

"Do you have a favorite flavor, Chase?" she asked.

"No. Not really. I could eat whatever. I'm not a huge cake person, honestly. It's up to you, Chi," Chase replied.

"Chi? That was my nickname when I was growing up. How did you know about that?"

"Uh…I really didn't know anything about it. It just came out, I guess," Chase answered. "You don't like it?"

"No, it's not that. It's just that no one other than Trey still calls me that, but I sort of like the way you say it better," Chivonne said, gazing into Chase's eyes.

"Oh, how's he doing? I haven't seen him since he came to church with you that one time."

"Trey is good. He travels so much for work, so he rarely has time to socialize. He did ask about you, talking about *'I hope that dude is treating you right, or I might have to run up on him!'*"

"Now that is hilarious! I knew he was looking at me cross-eyed!"

"Don't mind him. He looks at everyone cross-eyed, especially any new man that comes around me."

"It's all good, though. He's cool."

"Yeah, Trey acts like he's tough, but he's a really sweet guy. He's dating this new girl, though, and he seems to be pretty serious about her. I haven't met her yet, so I can't call it."

"That's cool that you two grew up looking out for each other like that. I bet he gave away a lot of good man secrets, huh?" Chase asked.

"Yeah, probably more than you guys would like us women to know," she answered.

"You know, I've been meaning to ask you something," he began.

"O…kay. What is it?"

"The day we met…the day I saw you at the market, sitting on the bench outside of the men's clothing store…were you with Trey that day?" he asked.

"It's funny that you ask! I was hoping that day that you hadn't seen me with him, just because I didn't want you to think that we were together...not that I was thinking that hard about you or anything," she said, nervously.

"Chivonne...it's cool. You don't have to hide the fact that you were mesmerized!" he teased.

Chase smiled, subtly, not taking his eyes off of her. She seemed to consent that she was mesmerized, keeping her eyes locked with his. After a few seconds, she looked down at the cake menu that she was holding, as the baker walked toward them.

"Do you have red velvet cake?" she asked the baker, looking up.

"Yes, Ms. Wilson, as a matter of fact we do! I'll go and get that from the kitchen so that you both can taste it. It's our best seller!"

As they waited for the baker to return, Chase felt like it was the best time to tell Chivonne his thoughts about having a big wedding, but he was afraid. He did not want to have a huge wedding, much less to be involved in planning it. Not wanting to ruin the mood, Chase was reluctant to be honest with her about his feelings, however, he knew he had to speak up if he was going to be a *happily* married man soon.

"Chivonne, can I be honest with you?"

"Of course, my love. What's on your mind?" she asked, smiling and turning towards him.

"With all of the wedding planning details we've been talking about lately, it has all reminded me that I really do not want a huge wedding and that wedding panning is really not my thing. I'm not into all the details like you women are. I know you probably want a huge wedding and would want me to be involved, but this is all very stressful for me, you know? My fiancé...*ex*-fiancé...and my mom planned this whole shindig that was just crazy to me, but that's what they wanted so I just went with it. But, can you and I just keep it simple and not go all wild and ridiculous with the wedding planning?"

"Chase, if it were up to me, I would have no more than ten people at our wedding. Believe it or not, I have not actually been planning my wedding since I was a little girl. I honestly could not care any less who comes to our wedding as long as I am marrying you."

"Really? I thought all women start planning their weddings when they are little girls…or at least that's what my sisters did!"

"That may be true, but I've never really been into that kind of thing. And, at my age, you kind of feel like you'll never meet somebody special enough to marry, so you kind of just want to get it over with once you do."

"You're not old, Chi, and there are plenty of women who have gotten married in their thirties…and in their forties, for that matter. But, honestly, I'm happy to know that we are on the same page as far as this wedding goes. That's one less thing that we'll have to sort through."

"You are absolutely right! That is one thing that we definitely do not have to argue about. Okay, let's just choose a cake and get out of here. Do you like red velvet?" Chivonne asked.

"If you want red velvet cake, I'm eating red velvet cake!" Chase answered.

"Well then, red velvet cake it is! Ma'am, we are going to go with red velvet cake with this design," Chivonne said to the baker, pointing to the picture of a white fondant cake design with turquoise lace embroidery and gold dust.

While Chivonne finalized cake plans with the bakery, Chase got up to browse around. After getting his worries off of his chest, he was relieved to discover that Chivonne wanted the same type of wedding that he wanted; small and simple. Learning to be completely honest with her took a huge weight off of his shoulders, but it was his mother that he had to deal with next. She hated red velvet cake.

12

July 31

"Go inside, man! Just go inside and tell her what's on your mind! It's not like you haven't had to talk to her about something serious before. You have spent your whole life taking on everyone else's issues and never dealing with your own. It's time out for that! Go inside!"

Chase coached himself out of his car, up to the house, and finally knocked on the door.

"I'm coming! Hold on a second." Mrs. Hendricks opened the door. "Hey baby, come on in," she yelled, walking back into the kitchen.

"Hey mom." Chase closed the door behind him and walked over to the couch to sit down.

"I just made some chicken and dumplings. Are you hungry?" she asked from the kitchen.

"No, thank you, I'm good. I had a big lunch at work today. I'll probably eat something later."

"Okay, well, if you change your mind, you are more than welcome to eat something."

"Thanks." Chase hesitated to get to what brought him to his mom's house that afternoon.

"What brings you here out of the blue, Chase?" she asked.

"I want to talk to you about Chivonne."

"What about her?" she asked, defensively.

"Well, about her being my wife soon and about you disrespecting our relationship."

"Chase! I am still your mother, no matter how grown you are or how many times you get engaged. Don't come for me when I haven't sent for you!"

"That's just it! You've been coming for Chivonne since the day you met her and she hasn't once sent for you, mom! And this has nothing to do with my engagement to Tamara…or does it?" he asked, hoping she would admit to it.

"Chase, everything was perfect. And for some reason unbeknownst to Tamara, or to me, you just up and dumped that child! And did you consult me? No. Not once!"

"That's because it wasn't your decision! It wasn't up to you whether or not she and I got married. It was no secret that you were more into that wedding than you were into her. Just admit that."

"Chase, if you came over here to chastise me for being involved in your wedding then you can leave! I was just trying to help! I will not stand here and let you belittle me. And you will not force me to like Chivonne!"

"You're right. I cannot force you to like her, but as her fiancé, it's my responsibility to protect our relationship. Yes, I am still part of this family, but I will have a new family soon, and I want to at least *start* on a good foot. If I start this marriage on the premise of me not standing up to anyone who speaks ill of my wife and our marriage, I'm pretty sure it won't end well. And, trust me. It would definitely *end* if I don't come correct!"

"Chase, I'm not going to argue with you about this, but what I will say is that you are rushing into this marriage. You two barely know each other, so you couldn't possibly know that you want to spend your life with her! That's just impossible and irresponsible," she answered.

"Okay. I don't want to argue with you either, but let me say this before I go." He stood up. "Pastor Young really been instrumental in helping us prepare for marriage. And if I remember correctly, he helped you and dad to keep your marriage together, right? Don't you think he can help us?" he asked, rhetorically. "Just think about that, mom. I'll see you later." He kissed his mom on her cheek and walked out.

NICOLE C DIGGS

13

August 8

"Hey Pastor Young, do you have a minute? Chivonne and I are headed to brunch, but I just wanted to talk to you for a second about something." Not giving him a chance to answer, Chase continued. "We told my family that we are engaged!" Chase began, hysterically. "They all hate Chivonne and everyone's saying that we are rushing and now I'm not sure about—"

"—Wait...wait...wait a minute, Chase! Slow down! Don't get ahead of yourself. Take a breath and *sloooowly* tell me what's going on."

"OK. Chivonne and I announced our engagement to my family, and honestly, they did not seem to take the news as well as I had imagined...my mom, especially. So I finally confronted her about how she has been acting when I bring Chivonne around the family, and she nearly disowned me, talking about *you don't even know that bougie girl*."

"OK. We'll get to that in a second. Just calm down. What about your dad?" Pastor Young asked.

"Thankfully, my dad loves Chivonne, now that he has gotten to know her, so he's been very supportive. At least I have him on my side, which helps, but you know how much my mom loved Tamara."

"Yes, I know. More so than you did. Go on."

"I honestly believe that she really does like Chivonne," Chase continued, "but, she is still upset with me about the fact that I did not marry Tamara. Not to mention, we decided on a small and private wedding, so my mom is obviously heated that she is not going to get to plan a wedding after all."

"OK. Stop right there. Chase, do you want to marry Chivonne?"

"Of course I want to marry her, and I will, but I've been having second thoughts about getting married so soon. I just don't know what to do at this point."

"Do you believe that God told you that Chivonne will be your wife?"

"Yes, absolutely. No question."

"Do you believe that God told you to propose to Chivonne when you did?"

"Absolutely. No question about it."

"Do you believe that your mother loves you?"

"Of course she does!"

"Then you will just have to trust God, son. You heard from God concerning your fiancé and how to move forward with that relationship. You know what He told you and how He orchestrated everything on your behalf. You know your mother loves you and only wants the best for you. You need to trust God and know what if you were obedient to Him, He will work it out. You know what God's word says. I don't have to tell you that, but if you need a reminder, here it is! Chase, all things work together for good to them that love God and are called according to His purpose. God's promise to you is His promise and will always be His promise. Regardless of what the situation looks like and how long you have to wait for your mother to come around, you have to trust God. That's your only responsibility. Just trust God."

"Okay." Chase had little else to say.

"Have you spoken to Chivonne about what's bothering you?"

"A little, but not really. Everything is going great with us and all the wedding planning, so I really just want to work it out myself and not burden her with my family issues."

"Chase, *she* will be your family in less than two months, so you may want to make a habit of telling her how you feel now. The single most important thing you need to learn about marriage is to communicate with your wife. Tell her everything, even if it makes one or both of you uncomfortable. Talk to her. Don't ever stop talking to her. Your pre-marital counseling begins soon, so get ready to open completely up. It will serve you good. It's all or nothing now."

"Don't keep your lovely lady waiting out there any longer," Pastor Young said, pushing Chase towards the exit door of his office. "Breathe, Chase. Trust God and breathe. Have a good afternoon, son,"

"You too, sir."

"Chase, talk to her," Pastor Young pointed at Chase with wide eyes.

"I will."

Being the oldest of four siblings, Chase had developed a bad habit of keeping things to himself. He never wanted to burden anyone else with his problems. From the day his mom told him that he was going to be a big brother and that he would be responsible for looking after his siblings, he had told himself that he had to hold in his own feelings and not trouble anyone with what he was going through. Chase knew that he needed to open up about what was going on in his mind, but he did not want to push Chivonne away. What Chase did not know was that she had been *waiting* for him to open up. She had always wanted a man who would be transparent with his feelings and brave enough to tackle any issue head on. Chase was unaware that she was stressing over the fact that they were planning to be married soon and they had not yet spoken openly about the night they announced their engagement to his family.

On the way to brunch, which had become their Sunday afternoon tradition, Chivonne snuck in a quick nap, while Chase drove in deep thought.

Once they arrived to and were seated at the restaurant, Chase excused himself to use the men's room. While Chase was away coaching himself back to the table, Chivonne pulled out her wireless phone to catch up on a few business e-mails.

"Okay, go back out there and just tell her what's on your mind. It's not that difficult, Chase! All you have to do is open your mouth and start talking! But, what if she doesn't understand or doesn't even want to hear about anything I'm going through? I don't want to ruin the afternoon by pouring out all of my problems on her. I'm sure she doesn't want to hear me whine. Just forget it. I'll bring it up another time." Realizing how long he had been in the men's room, Chase quickly walked back to the table.

"What were you doing in there, Chase? I thought you jumped out of the window or something," Chivonne laughed.

"Yeah, sorry about that," Chase said, looking away.

"Is everything okay?" she asked.

"Yeah, yeah. Everything is good. Did you order yet?" he rushed.

"No, I didn't order yet. I was waiting on you. I wasn't sure if you wanted your usual or if you were in the mood for something different today. Oh, I did order you a cranberry juice, though…with extra ice! See, Chase, I know you like the back of my hand now!" Chivonne could sense that everything was, in fact, *not* good with Chase, but she wanted him to initiate conversation about it, instead of her digging for details.

"Yes, thank you. Cranberry juice with extra ice. You know me too well."

Once the waitress arrived to take their orders, Chase signaled for

Chivonne to order first as he pulled out his own phone, attempting to settle his mind. Chase then placed his order and Chivonne went back to checking her emails, looking up only to thank the waitress for bringing her food to the table and to take a sip of her water.

After their food arrived, Chase sat quietly in front of his plate, glancing around the restaurant, still arguing with himself about the conversation that he was avoiding.

"Now's your chance, man! Talk to her! This is your future wife. Whatever you have to tell her, she can handle it. God brought you two together so you need to trust that he will work it out."

"Chivonne, I need to talk to you about something," he blurted out.

"Okay," she responded, looking around to see if Chase had drawn attention to their table. "What's going on?"

"So…my mom is upset about our engagement. Well, not really about the engagement itself, but the fact that it happened so quickly. Everyone is saying we are rushing into this. You know I love you so very much and I know that God brought us together. You know I want you to be my wife, but do you think maybe we are moving just a little too fast?"

Surprised by what he said, Chivonne did not know how to respond, although she was relieved that Chase had finally broken the silence. She was ready to walk the rest of the way with him.

"Chase, I love you like I have never loved any man before…like I've never loved *anyone* before. I trust you and I know that you love me, too. Most of all, I trust God and I know that what God promised us will happen in our lives. Regardless of who may put their negative words on our relationship, this relationship is between only three people: you, God, and me. No one else matters. People around us are going to question our relationship because they don't understand what God has promised us. They have not been through what we each have been through, and they don't understand how everything could happen so fast. But, all we can do is trust God, Chase. We have to trust that he has prepared us and brought us together for a greater purpose than just our relationship and that he will use our lives and marriage as a testimony of his love. We have to know that regardless of what people may think or say about us, we are following God. Chase, just trust God."

"Pastor Young said the same exact thing to me." Chase said, under his breath, without looking up at her.

So much had to be discussed between them and Chase was finally ready to talk. He was relieved that Chivonne was able to handle it all and she was happy that he finally opened up. They both knew that communication between them was going to be the key to unlock the trust and comfort they needed from each other. Communication was what would draw them closer to each other and make things even more clear as they quickly moved forward.

14

Three weeks later

"Good evening Pastor Young. How are you? And how is the Mrs.?" Chivonne asked Pastor Young, as she hugged him.

"Everything is good, Chivonne. The wife is good. And when everything with the wife is good, life is good! Chase will have to learn that very soon!" he said, winking at Chase.

"Oh, now I am ready to experience *all* the perks of being married! We haven't covered that yet! But, last' week's session was really eye-opening and I think we've done well, wouldn't you say?" Chivonne asked Pastor Young.

"Oh, absolutely! In fact…and this stays in this room…the two of you have made more progress in your relationship and in pre-marital counseling in less than a month than most of the married couples that come into my office do their entire lives! And that is exactly what I want us to talk about for our last session tonight. Let's all have a seat and get comfortable, and we'll get started," he said, pointing to the chairs in front of his desk.

Chivonne took her seat and Chase sat down after pulling his chair in a bit closer to hers, putting his arm around the back of her chair.

"And how are you, Chase? Are you ready to roll tonight?" he asked.

"I am ready to roll, Pastor! Most definitely," he answered.

"Alright, good. So, let's pray first and then we'll begin." They each bowed their heads. "Dear Lord, we want to thank you for your love and your grace that you show us every day. We do not take for granted that you give us the opportunity to see another day and to continue learning more about you and about your will for us. Thank you for this lovely couple that is soon to be married. I thank you because they know that they are in your will and that you have put them together to fulfill something much greater than them. We give you honor for being the head of our lives and leading us into your will for our lives. We thank you for what you will teach Chivonne and Chase tonight as they prepare for the best years of their lives together as husband and wife. In Jesus' name we pray. Amen."

"Amen," Chivonne and Chase repeated, in unison.

"Chase, I want to begin with you."

"Okay."

"When you hear the word intentional, what does that mean to you in regards to your relationships, whether it be with Chivonne or someone else?"

"Okay. For me, being intentional means first of all knowing what I want in life or in my relationship with her and knowing the purpose of our relationship. I understand that God does not put people together just for the sake of them being together, but it's for a reason. Whether that reason is to be an example to others of God's love for his children, or to be leaders of a church, or to travel the world together and share the gospel, fulfilling our purpose together is more important than us just seeing each other every day. People get married every day, but what impact are they having on the world together, you know? That's the beginning of being intentional; knowing the purpose of marriage, knowing our purpose together, knowing what we both want out of the relationship and growing together in order to reach those goals."

"Thank you, Chase, for that sermon!" Pastor Young interjected. "I did not intend for it to be as super spiritual as you made it, but that's good! Knowing your purpose together as far as ministry goes is super important. Chivonne, how about you?"

"Well...to me...being intentional in my relationship with

Chase, and with everyone really, means that I'll only do or say things that will help us get to a certain place in our relationship. It means that I will avoid, or try to avoid doing certain things that I know will not help us grow individually and as a couple, like Chase said. We have to know what we want in life and in our relationship, and intentionally go after that."

"Awesome! Those were both great answers. Now, I want to add to that the need to learn about each other in an effort to recognize if the other person has the same goals for life and if he or she is truly what we need in order to be better individuals. Yes, marriage is about fulfilling a purpose together, but it is also about two imperfect people coming together to intentionally help each other grow and mature individually. I'll give you an example. Chivonne may have a rough day at work and come home tired and ready to go to bed. But you, Chase, may have had an amazing day and are full of joy. In the past, you may have been accustomed to being by yourself and avoiding someone when he or she is in a bad mood, but you may have to put on your selfless hat and help her get out of that mood without forcing your own happiness onto her. Whether or not we like it or even recognize it when it happens, our spouses indirectly teach us how to be patient, how to love despite the issues that may arise, how to be kind even when the other person is getting on our nerves and how to be giving, even when the other person does not seem to be appreciative. Our spouses unintentionally teach us, on a daily basis, how to be more like Christ and more like who God created us to be. But, we have to be more intentional about how we choose to handle those challenging situations. So, what I want you both to do now is to think about a time in your relationship when you had to deal with the other person's feelings and how you did not handle it too well. Think about how you responded. Did you tear the other person down? Did you condemn the other person for not being perfect in that moment? Think about the outcome that you would have wanted and how you could be intentional in order to get to that outcome."

Pastor Young went on to share his own experience with being intentional in his marriage, as well as with being a pastor. They each discussed their own situations, and shared how they would have handled them differently, had they been more intentional about what they wanted to solve in those moments.

"Before we end, I just want to say something to Chase, if that is okay," Chivonne interjected.

"Sure, that's perfectly okay. Go ahead, Chivonne," Pastor Young replied.

"This may not be the best place to say this, but I want to say it before we go any further." She turned towards Chase.

Chase's eyes opened wide, as if he had just seen a ghost. "What?" he asked.

"Chase, umm, I was the one who stood you up on that blind date that you went on the night before we met! I'm so sorry!"

"Wow! That is funny, Chivonne! I definitely thought you were about to drop a bomb on me just now. Don't scare me like that, girl! Besides, I kind of thought so when I saw you having lunch with my co-worker, Kye, the week after that. How long have you known this? Did she tell you?"

"No, Kye didn't tell me. She doesn't even know we're together. I guess I sort of figured it out on my own. Remember when you told me that you had seen me before and I asked you why you never said anything to me?" she asked.

"Yeah, I remember that."

"So, after that, you told me that you had been ditched for a blind date that your co-worker set up the night before we met. And since you said it had you bummed out and that the girl was rude for standing you up, I didn't want to admit to it. So, since we are being completely honest, I figured I wanted to tell you right now that it was me who stood you up!" she smiled, hoping that she did not upset him.

"That's pretty wild, Chi! I guess God would not let you stand in your own way. We were bound to meet each other, no matter how hard we tried not to," he answered.

"Chase, I just want to say thank you," she continued. "You have been everything I've ever wanted during this entire process. From the day we met, you showed me that you were genuinely interested, not just because you saw a pretty girl, but because you saw *me*, and you were interested in *me*. Somehow you saw who I was inside and you knew what you wanted. Just like we talked about tonight, you knew that you wanted to make me your wife and you were intentional with me. I was so used to guys only wanting to take me out because of what I had or because I was just another nice girl they met on a blind date or because I am successful, but you didn't care about any of that. You only cared about finding out about my life and how I became who I am as a person. You cared about making me part of your own life. So, with Pastor Young as my witness,, I promise to try and give back to you everything you've given me and to be the best wife I can possibly be to you. I may not always get it right and I'm pretty sure I'll frustrate you sometimes or disappoint you, but I promise to try every day to get better and to make you happy."

Grabbing her hand from her lap, Chase moved in closer to her as he began to speak. "Chivonne, you don't have to try to make me happy. As long as you give me the honor of being your husband for rest of our lives, I will always be happy with you."

"I know I don't have to try so hard Chase, but I just want to tell you what's on my mind. In just a short time, pre-marital counseling has really helped me to understand how to see that even though we have different perspectives on many different topics, we can still love and respect each other. Regardless of what goes on around or between us, we can still be happy. Every week I learned something new about you, and myself, too. I learned that I can disagree with you and still love you enough to not argue with you about our disagreements. I also learned a hard lesson about how to consider you when making decisions, which has been particularly difficult for me since I've been independent for so long."

"I appreciate you, Chi," Chase began. "And, although it has been hard for me, I had to accept the fact that you often have stressful workdays, and you need time to yourself to relax after work instead of giving me all of your free time. That's hard! I always want to spend every moment with you!"

"Aww, Chase. You're so sweet. I'm so glad that God brought you into my life. I'll tell you one thing. I couldn't have chosen a better man for myself, that's for sure! I've waited for what seemed like an eternity to spend every moment with *you*."

Chase stood up and pulled Chivonne out of her chair. He grabbed her arms and wrapped them around his waist. Pulling her in close to him, he wrapped his arms around her shoulders, holding her tightly.

Pastor Young stood by, smiling, with his hands clasped in front of him. "Okay love birds. Let's get out of here, shall we?" he joked.

As Chivonne and Chase reluctantly let each other loose, they grabbed their belongings and made their way outside of the office, with Pastor Young following.

What they had learned in that session was that it was vital to the success of their relationship that they allowed themselves and each other to be open about everything. They learned to embrace accountability and guidance from Pastor Young's counseling, as well as the support of friends and family.

15

Later that night

Much to their surprise, Chase's mom had called Chase and suggested that they meet for dinner. They decided it would be a good a idea to meet at a nearby restaurant after their counseling session.

Chivonne and Chase had come to understand how important counseling was for their relationship, but what pre-marital counseling did not do was change Chase's mom's mind about the upcoming wedding—that was between her and God. As Chivonne and Chase grew closer to each other, Chase's mom had pulled further and further away from him—or so it seemed.

As they pulled up to the restaurant, Chivonne was hesitant to go inside.

"What's wrong, Chi?" Chase asked.

"I don't know about this, Chase. From the way she was acting the last time I saw her, I am not sure I want to be sitting across from her with knives and forks and glass on the table! This could get ugly!" Chivonne said, jokingly.

"Seriously, Chivonne? What do you think will happen? You think she'll cut you or something?" Chase asked, laughing out loud.

Not amused, she rolled her eyes at him. "I don't know *what* she'll do. But, what I do know is that she doesn't like me and I'm uncomfortable just thinking about it."

"Chivonne, get out of the car please," Chase said, impatiently. "Just come on inside. My mother is not going to kill you. Don't make me have to get churchy on you—"

"That won't be necessary, Chase," cutting him off. "I know that *God has not given me the spirit of fear...*" she chanted, as if she were holding a Bible in front of her and reading from it.

"Exactly! And don't you forget it. Now, we've prayed and fasted and did all that good stuff to make sure we are following God's lead, and he will not let us down! Sure, we have our own thoughts about how my mother has been acting and we *think* we know what she has been thinking, but we don't know anything for sure because she hasn't told us. And here, God has given us this grand opportunity to possibly finally understand her point of view and you're letting fear paralyze you? Absolutely not! I won't allow it. So, we are going to get out of this car and go inside this restaurant and sit across from my scary mother and hear what she has to say. And then we are going to respond to her, if we need to, even if she tries to cut you!"

Chase was frustrated with the entire ordeal, but he had had enough with fear getting the best of them both, when it came to dealing with his mom and his relationship.

As they were getting out of the car, Chase's dad yelled from across the parking lot to catch their attention. "I thought that was your car, son. Come on inside." As the four of them walked into the restaurant, they greeted one another as they waited to be seated. Chase made small talk with his mom, and Chivonne felt more comfortable chatting with his dad. As Chivonne and Chase sat down next to each other first, Chivonne noticed Chase's mom pulled her husband aside, whispering and motioning to let her sit across from Chivonne and for him to sit across from Chase. Chivonne and Chase quickly glanced at each other in slight unease, having no idea what was about to happen.

"So, how was your ride over here? Did you find the place okay?" Chase's dad asked Chivonne, breaking the silence.

"It was a rather quick ride. We came straight over after our premarital counseling session ended. Today was the last session!" Chivonne said, excitedly.

"Oh, nice! That must have been exciting and grueling, I can imagine," Mr. Hendricks replied, grinning.

"Oh, absolutely. It was intense, and extremely helpful…and trying, but very necessary. Eye-opening, too. But, you know what? It helped that Chase knows Pastor Young personally and that I actually met him before we started counseling."

"Absolutely! Pastor Young is a great counselor. He's a very good friend of ours, actually. He's known Chase since he was just an ashy young boy!" Chase's dad replied. Everyone chuckled.

As Chivonne and Mr. Hendricks ended their small talk from across the table, Chase did everything he could to avoid eye contact with his mom. Mustering up all of the guts he had, he eventually broke the silence between them.

"So, mom…how has your week been so far?" Chase asked.

"It has been blessed, son. Thank you for asking. And what about you?"

"It has been good. Chivonne and I are excited about the wedding. It's just fifteen days from now, so we've been tying some loose ends this week," looking over at Chivonne, "and before you know it, we'll be husband and wife, and you know what *that* means! Hint, hint," Chase said, winking and elbowing Chivonne in her side.

"WHAT?" they all shouted in unison.

Chase, trying to appear innocent, replied, "well…that means that we will be…uh…starting our lives together."

"Oh, okay. If you say so, son," his mom replied, shocked that he had the guts to even imply. It was apparent by everyone's reactions that they knew exactly what he meant.

"Honey, the marriage bed is undefiled, so let them young folks do what they wanna do when the get married!" Mr. Hendricks exclaimed to his wife. "And mind your business about it!"

"Anyway," Chase's mom interjected, "what we invited you both to dinner for tonight is to talk to you about a few things. Well...me...in particular."

Chivonne quickly looked over at Chase and noticed his raised eyebrows, as he was surprised that his mom jumped right into it. Looking back over to Chase's mom, Chivonne slowly grabbed Chase's hand underneath the table, holding on tightly, reminding him that they were in this thing together, no matter what his mom had to say.

"Chivonne, I'll start with you," she began.

"Mom!" Chase shouted.

"Son, just wait a minute. Let me say what I have to say. You've been waiting for me to talk about this, so let me talk, if that's okay with you. Now hush!" She continued. "Chivonne, I want to first apologize to you for the way I have been behaving since the day we met. I don't know you and you don't know me, but I can see that we do have at least one thing in common—we both love my son. Now, I will admit that I was surprised that the two of you were engaged after just three short months of knowing each other, so I had to get down on my knees and pray. And when I say pray, I mean I had to get down on my knees and talk to God for myself! Anyway, while I was doing all that praying and talking to God, I was not listening to him. I prayed that God would open up your eyes for you to see that you were moving too fast, but what I needed was for God to open *my* eyes. As much as I didn't want to admit it to Chase when he came to talk to me, I realize that he was right and I was out of line. I've been sitting back and watching this relationship grow and now I see clearly that God is the reason you two are together. And, because I know my son and what he has been through, I know that you came along at the perfect time, Chivonne. And, as much as I wanted Chase to marry that other young girl, I know it was only because I wanted to plan the wedding. She wasn't right for him, but I didn't want to accept it at first. I was being selfish. I made it more about myself having the chance to plan the wedding I never had, but I now realize that it wasn't about me. And *your* relationship is not about me either. It is not easy to say any of this, but I just want to say that I'm sorry if I pushed you away and made you feel unwelcomed in my house and into this family."

Both Chivonne and Chase were speechless. Chase glared at his mom in astonishment. Chivonne stared at Chase, hoping he would speak first. Chase's dad issued his glances like clockwork around the table. Even he was shocked that those words came from the wife he's known for almost forty years. Chase's mom waited patiently for anyone to say something—anything.

Chase's dad spoke up, breaking the silence—yet again. "Soooo, anyone got any room for dessert?" he said slowly, easing into it.

Chivonne spoke first. "Mrs. Hendricks, I really appreciate your honesty. I know that it could not have been easy to watch Chase move into a new relationship so quickly, so I can understand why you may have felt the way that you did. All I ever wanted was for you to give me a chance—to give *us* a chance. As badly as I wanted to, I also realized that I could not make you like me or make you see that God brought us together exactly the way he wanted to. That was between you and God. So, I'm glad that you allowed God to change your heart an I'm so happy that you are able to see that now! So, thank you for that. Thank God for that!" Chivonne was relieved at Mrs. Hendricks' apology, yet she was still holding on tightly to Chase's hand.

"Mom, thank you. That's all I can say. Thank you. And, thank you Lord!" Chase yelled, as he shook his finger towards the ceiling.

As they finished their meals, they chatted about wedding details and caught Chase's parents up to all they had missed over the last few weeks. Chase's mom, especially, had a lot of catching up to do.

Chivonne and Chase spent the ride back to her apartment talking about the conversation that happened at dinner. When they pulled up in front of the apartment building, Chase asked Chivonne to wait before getting out of the car to go inside.

"Can I talk to you before you go?" he asked.

"Sure. What's on your mind?" she asked.

"I love you," he said, gently grabbing her hand, looking softly into her eyes. "I mean, *for real for real.* I love everything about you. I love your smile. I love your hair. I love your personality. I love your sense of humor. I love your passion for life. You're so beautiful to me! But, most of all, I love your faith in God. I love how you trusted God to bring us together and how you trust him to *keep* us together. My family is crazy, but you held on through all the craziness that's happened over the past few months! You didn't let their negativity push you away from me or away from what God was and *is* doing in our lives. You had so many opportunities to run, but you didn't. You stayed right here with me through every minute of the madness, and I'm so glad that God chose me to be your husband."

16

As the wedding soon approached, Chivonne and Chase spent the last days leading up to their wedding talking about everything they had learned in pre-marital counseling and how they would apply it all to their marriage. Chivonne expressed to Chase that she came to understand the reason why she had to wait as long as she had waited to be married. She shared with Chase the word that was spoken over her life many years ago.

Chivonne recognized that her period of waiting was not a result of God not wanting her to be married, but it was the time that he was preparing her to be able to handle everything that happened over the last few months. During her time of waiting, God was growing her, showing her how to love, teaching her how to be selfless and giving, teaching her how to be intentional in her relationships, leading her into her purpose, and preparing her for the tests that she and Chase would face during their engagement.

She had spent many years in preparation for how her life would change in a matter of months. Her faith was challenged. Her willingness to hold on to a promise from God was tested. She wanted to give up. She wanted to give up her hopes of being married one day, because waiting for that day was challenging.

Watching Chase go through so much was tough for her, but she was prepared and ready to fight for her promise from God; the promise that God would send her a husband, and that she would not have to look for him—she would have to wait for him to find her.

More importantly, God wanted Chivonne to spend all of those years of waiting with him. He wanted her to get to know him, get to know his love, and get to know his voice. He wanted all of her.

As she reflected back on all of the years she spent praying for a husband, she realized that God did not have her full attention. She had become so focused on "being found" that she had not pursued God and her own passion and purpose, and allowed her husband to find her in God. God also let her in on a little secret; her marriage would be an example of a Godly marriage and a testament of true love because she waited on God for Chase to find and pursue her. She believed that God would give her every desire of her heart concerning marriage and that he would make good on every promise that he made. She had resolved that if she had to wait any longer, she was willing to. Becoming Mrs. Chase Hendricks was God's promise to her and her dream come true. Chase was worth playing the waiting game.